BONNIE JACK

IAN HAMILTON

BONNIE JACK

A

ANANSI

Published in Canada in 2021 and the USA in 2021 by House of Anansi Press Inc.
www.houseofanansi.com

House of Anansi Press is committed to protecting our natural environment. This book is made of material from well-managed FSC®-certified forests, recycled materials, and other controlled sources.

House of Anansi Press is a Global Certified Accessible™ (GCA by Benetech) publisher. The ebook version of this book meets stringent accessibility standards and is available to students and readers with print disabilities.

25 24 23 22 21   1 2 3 4 5

Library and Archives Canada Cataloguing in Publication

Title: Bonnie Jack / Ian Hamilton.
Names: Hamilton, Ian, 1946– author.
Identifiers: Canadiana (print) 2020039374X | Canadiana (ebook) 20200393782 |
ISBN 9781487007089 (softcover) | ISBN 9781487007096 (EPUB) |
ISBN 9781487007102 (Kindle)
Classification: LCC PS8615.A4423 B66 2021 | DDC C813/.6—dc23

Cover and text design: Alysia Shewchuk
Typesetting: Lucia Kim

House of Anansi Press respectfully acknowledges that the land on which we operate is the Traditional Territory of many Nations, including the Anishinabeg, the Wendat, and the Haudenosaunee. It is also the Treaty Lands of the Mississaugas of the Credit.

 Canada Council   Conseil des Arts
for the Arts   du Canada

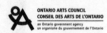 ONTARIO ARTS COUNCIL
CONSEIL DES ARTS DE L'ONTARIO
an Ontario government agency
un organisme du gouvernement de l'Ontario

With the participation of the Government of Canada
Avec la participation du gouvernement du Canada | Canadä

We acknowledge for their financial support of our publishing program the Canada Council for the Arts, the Ontario Arts Council, and the Government of Canada.

Printed and bound in Canada

MIX
Paper from
responsible sources
FSC® C103567
www.fsc.org

Dedicated to the memory of my father, William. Known to his friends in Canada as Bill, his friends in Scotland as Willie, and to my mother as Jock. Whatever the name and wherever he was, he was a man who struggled mightily to escape his demons and never could.

Prologue

Glasgow, Scotland
November 1934

SHE SAT IN THE cinema between her two children, her well-worn wool coat musty and damp from the rain. The children had thought they were going out to the shops, but to their delight she had taken them to the Regal Cinema for the Saturday afternoon matinee.

"If we go in here, you can't tell your father about this. You have to promise me," their mother had said earlier as they stood at the ticket window.

"I promise," the girl, nine, and the boy, six, chorused.

"Cross your hearts," their mother said.

Both children dutifully crossed their hearts.

There were no ice creams or lollies for them, and they had to kneel on their seats to see past the heads that towered in front, but they didn't care, as they had John Wayne and Tim McCoy to entertain them. John came first in *The Lucky Texan*. It didn't matter to the children if he was a great actor; it was enough that he was a cowboy on the open range. What could possibly be more exotic to small children living in the Gorbals neighbourhood of Glasgow, one of the most densely populated and poorest parts of the British kingdom?

When the first film ended, the mother said to her son, "I have to take Moira to the loo. Will you be all right by yourself for five minutes?"

"I'll be fine, Mummy," he said.

She leaned over and kissed him on the forehead. "I love you so much," she said.

The Tim McCoy film began before his mother and sister returned, and he was soon caught up in it. About halfway through he realized they still hadn't come back. He wondered briefly where they were but then thought maybe his sister wasn't feeling well, and returned to the movie. It wasn't until it ended and the people around him began to file out of the cinema that he felt a touch of fear. Still, he sat and he waited, sure his mother would come to get him when the aisles cleared.

She didn't.

He slumped in the seat, his head not visible above its back, and he began to cry. The cleaning staff discovered him as they swept up the litter.

"Who brought you here?" a woman asked.

"My mum."

"Where is she?"

"She took my sister to the loo and she hasn't come back."

"I'm sure she'll be back soon enough."

His crying intensified.

"Laddie, I told you she'll be back."

"But she left after the John Wayne film," he said between sobs.

The woman looked at him and then turned to speak to a woman working several rows in front. "Sadie, look after this wee laddie for a few minutes. I need to go find his mum."

The boy closed his eyes, trying to fight back the tears.

"Don't cry," the other woman said. "We'll find your mum."

Moira must be sick, he thought.

But the woman didn't return, and he began to hear voices at the rear of the cinema. One of those voices was the cleaning woman's, and it kept saying "poor wee laddie."

Tears flowed again, and this time he gave in to them completely.

1

Wellesley Hills, Massachusetts
November 1988

ANNE AND JACK ANDERSON's children began to gather at the family home in Wellesley Hills the day before Thanksgiving.

Late on Wednesday morning, their oldest son, Brent, arrived by car from New York City with his wife, Maggie, and their six-month-old daughter, Ainsley. Brent was an investment banker with a large international firm. He was the closest temperamentally to his father, and when he married, Anne had worried about how his unwillingness to display emotion would play out with Maggie, an effusive young woman who wore her heart on her sleeve. Six years later, the marriage seemed to be strong, even though neither of them had apparently changed their natural disposition.

Their other son, Mark, flew into Boston from Chicago, where he worked as a commodities trader. Anne drove to

Logan Airport to meet him and her daughter, Allison, who was arriving later in the day from Los Angeles. Whatever concerns Anne had about Brent were doubled when it came to Mark. His job was stressful, and he obsessed about it day and night. An early marriage had lasted barely six months, and two live-in girlfriends had come and gone since then. He claimed that their home in Wellesley Hills was the only place where he could truly feel calm. Anne hoped it wouldn't take him the entire five days of his stay to relax.

Mark arrived at two and sat with Anne as they waited for Allison and her husband's plane. When she asked him about his work, he waved his hand in the air and said, "I don't have to think about it until Monday, so I don't want to talk about it. And you can do me a favour and ask Dad not to quiz me about it either."

They sat side by side on a bench. Her arm was looped through his, and she gently rubbed his forearm. "I'll tell him, but you know he doesn't always listen."

"How is he doing anyway? What does he have, about nine months to go before retirement?"

"His last day is officially August 31, but he has months of holiday and sick leave accumulated. I've been trying to get him to use it so he can leave earlier."

"Will he?"

"What do you think?"

"He'll leave August 31 and not a day sooner," Mark said.

"That's a very good guess."

"I wish he'd start to wean himself from Pilgrim. If he doesn't, the suddenness of not going in to work every day is going to come as one hell of a shock," Mark said. "How many years has he been there?"

"Almost forty, and as president for the last twenty," Anne said. "As for weaning, that doesn't seem to be in his plans. When it comes to that company, he doesn't know how to give anything less than one hundred percent. It's been like that since the beginning, and I guess it will end the same way."

"He's had a great run. It took that kind of work ethic, and foresight and guts, to take a regional player like Pilgrim and turn it into a national power. I have colleagues in Chicago who are careful when they deal with me simply because I'm Bloody Jack Anderson's son."

"You know he dislikes being referred to as Bloody Jack."

"I know, but it is what everyone calls him, and they have their reasons. I know it must be difficult for you to think of Dad as ruthless, but that's how he's regarded by many. He has never been sentimental about any part of Pilgrim and he's never been afraid to make hard decisions when they're needed. In business those are terrific attributes. Besides, who can argue with his success, or the respect he generates?"

"I've never once thought of your father as ruthless."

"Neither have I, but I understand that Pilgrim's Jack Anderson and my father Jack Anderson can form two parts of the same man. Anyway, in my mind, Dad is just a smart, hard-nosed executive who does what he thinks is necessary for the good of the business and its shareholders. This country would be better off if there were more men like him."

"All that may be true, but he still hates that nickname."

Mark looked towards the gate from which Allison, her husband, Tony, and their three-year-old son, Jonathan, were scheduled to emerge. "I don't want to harp on this, but aren't you worried that Dad's transition to retirement could be rocky?" he asked his mother.

"I didn't say I'm not worried, but this is your father we're talking about. He might have plans he hasn't discussed with me yet."

"What's he going to do? Take up golf or tennis? It's a bit late for new hobbies."

"Your father has never had a hobby, and I can't imagine him starting now," she said. "I assume he'll serve on some corporate boards and perhaps become involved in charitable work."

"He'll get plenty of invitations to join boards, I'm sure."

"Then there you are. Those will keep him busy."

Mark smiled and pointed towards the gate. "And there is Allison," he said. His sister—a lanky five foot ten with a mop of frizzy auburn hair—wasn't hard to pick out in a crowd.

It took close to an hour for Allison and Tony to retrieve their bags, and another fifteen minutes for Anne to find the car and get out of the parking lot. There was a flurry of conversation in the car as Anne, Mark, Allison, and

Tony got caught up on each other's lives, but when the car exited the Mass Pike and started along Route 9, the talk dwindled. When they reached Cliff Road and began the climb to Pierce, the chit-chat ended altogether. There was something about coming home — to their home, to the grandest home in the wealthiest neighbourhood of Boston's toniest commuter town — that filled the children with a need to take it all in quietly.

When the car rounded the corner onto Monadnock, Allison nudged her son and he turned to look out the window. "There's our house, just like I told you," she said to him. "See all those candles in the windows and the wreath on the door? Grandma always makes this house so special for the holidays."

The house was constructed of brown brick, with oak trim and a slate roof. It was set back fifty yards from the road, on the crest of a hillock. A stone-paved semicircular driveway ran up to it, past a lawn flanked by rows of carefully tended flowerbeds and bushes, many of which had retained some colour in the unseasonably warm fall. The house had two storeys, with six windows on the upper floor facing the road, and two huge windows on either side of a bright red double door on the ground floor. Ten wide stone steps climbed from the driveway to the door. Two pillars, each with a carved stone lion perched on top, sat at the base of the steps. A three-car garage, separated from the house by a laneway, stood off to the right. In front of the garage was the family Mercedes-Benz sedan and a Subaru that belonged to Brent.

"It always looks so welcoming," Allison said.

"It's our home, and it's still your home whenever you want it to be," Anne said.

"I've always thought it's like a castle sitting on top of a mountain," Mark said.

"I said the same thing to your father the first time I saw it," Anne said. "Which almost discouraged him from buying it."

"Why?" Tony asked.

"Jack dislikes ostentatious display, and he thought it was a bit too grand," she said. "But I had done my research, so I told him it was built by a Boston fish merchant who had six children and needed a good-sized home."

"Maybe he needed the seven bedrooms and four bathrooms, but what about the dining room that can seat thirty, the library, the tennis court, the patio with its own kitchen, and the swimming pool with a cabana about the size of my apartment in Chicago?" Mark said with a smile.

"I know it's large, but we don't have a cottage on the Cape or a chalet in Vermont," Anne said.

"Don't pay any attention to him, Mom," Allison said. "He loves this place as much as any of us."

"I most certainly do," Mark said.

The car turned into the driveway. Before it could come to a stop, the front door opened and Brent and Maggie appeared. As soon as Anne had parked the car, Allison leapt out and ran up the steps towards them. She threw her arms around Brent and was immediately joined in a group hug by Maggie.

Mark turned to Tony and Jonathan. "We sure are a huggy family," he said.

"I like hugs," Jonathan said.

"And so you should," Anne said, smiling broadly as she looked at her children. Nothing made her happier than seeing them all together.

"You have such a wonderful family," Tony said, as if reading her mind.

"Present company excluded," Mark said.

Tony leaned towards him. "No, Mark, you're as big a part of it as anyone. Let me tell you something. We're producing a film right now about the machinations of the financial markets, and one of the key characters is a hard-nosed trader who surprises his more cynical colleagues with his honesty and ethics. That character is based to a large extent on you."

"Tony, what a lovely thing to say!" Anne said.

"It's only the truth."

"Thanks," Mark said rather awkwardly. "I do like to think of myself as being honest. It's something Dad drilled into all of us."

"Speaking of Jack, where is he?" Tony asked.

"He won't be home yet," Anne said.

"But it's the day before Thanksgiving."

"When did that ever make a difference? The office closes at five, and that's when he'll leave."

Mark and Tony carried the luggage into the house, stopping to share more hugs at the door. Anne trailed after them with Jonathan. "Dinner is at seven, but we'll feed Jonathan and Ainsley earlier," she said. "After the rest of you have settled, we can meet in the kitchen for drinks."

"What's for dinner?" Mark asked.

"What would you expect in this house on the night before Thanksgiving?"

"Lasagna, a Caesar salad with anchovies on the side, and loaves of warm garlic bread," he said.

"Then you won't be disappointed."

"Do you need any help with dinner?" Allison asked.

"All I need to do is warm up the lasagna and bread and mix the salad, but we can do it together."

While the new arrivals went to their rooms, Brent and Maggie began to open the bottles of wine that Anne had left on the sideboard in the kitchen. If the Andersons had a discernible weakness, it was alcohol in its various forms. Most of them drank wine, but Anne liked gin martinis, her husband drank Scotch, and Mark preferred beer.

While the drinks were being organized, Anne put the finishing touches on a cheeseboard. She placed it, a plate of crackers, and a basket of warm baguette slices in the middle of the two-hundred-year-old pine rectory table she'd bought three months after moving to Wellesley, at a farmhouse sale near Weston. The table had no chairs to go with it, so Anne had two twelve-foot pine benches made by a local carpenter. The table and benches had been in constant use ever since, the place where the family gathered to eat, drink, and talk. An even-larger antique Regency oak table with eight legs, brass-capped feet, and twenty-four padded chairs sat in the dining room. It was used only at Christmas and Thanksgiving and for entertaining large groups.

It was just past five o'clock when they all assembled in the kitchen. After the children were fed and the first drinks were poured, the family sat around the table in their well-established positions. Anne, as always, played the role of instigator, asking questions that she already knew the answers to but stimulating discussion. Drinks flowed and time passed quickly as the Anderson children and their partners talked about the past year. It had been successful in different ways for all of them, so there was lots to tell and a receptive audience to tell it to.

As Brent was recounting a story about a deal he'd closed in London, Allison looked at her watch. "Mom, it's almost six-thirty. Where's Dad? He should be home by now."

"I'm sure traffic was difficult in the city, and the Mass Pike will be busy."

"How long will the lasagna take to heat?"

"About an hour. We can put it in now, if you want."

"Let's do that."

At seven o'clock there was still no sign of Jack Anderson, and Anne began to fret. By seven-thirty, as Allison and Maggie were taking the lasagna and bread out of the oven, she was really beginning to worry. "This isn't like your father. He always calls if he's going to be this late," she said.

"I'm sure he's sitting on the Mass Pike in the middle of a traffic jam," Allison said.

"Well, we can't wait for him. I don't want this food to get cold," Anne said.

Dinner was laid out on the sideboard and everyone began to serve themselves. Mark went last, and just as he was setting his plate on the table, there was a noise at the front door.

Anne stood up. "It's your father," she said, and left the table.

Anne, like her daughter, was tall and lean. Her long, thin face had a pointed nose, a sharp chin, and clearly defined cheekbones. She could have looked imperious, maybe even harsh, but her appearance was softened by a curly mass of blonde hair and large blue-green eyes that usually radiated kindness and concern. Not this night.

"Where were you?" she said sharply to her husband. "We've already started dinner."

Standing six foot four, Jack towered over her. He held out his arms and she stepped into them tentatively. "I'm sorry. I had an unexpected last-minute meeting."

"On the night before Thanksgiving?"

"It wasn't scheduled, but I had to take it."

She gazed up at him. Jack was sixty but looked fifty. His face was as finely hewn as hers, but his chin was square, not sharp, and where her skin was beginning to crease, his was still taut. The only real sign of ageing was the silver streaks running through his full head of black hair, which he combed straight back.

"You should have phoned," Anne said.

"I know. I'm sorry, I was distracted."

"And you've been drinking. I can smell it on your breath."

"It was that kind of meeting."

"Is everything okay?"

"It couldn't be better," he said. "Now don't keep me standing by the door. I'd like to see the kids."

"C'mon," she said, finally smiling.

Jack took off his tie and undid the top button of his shirt as he walked towards the kitchen. "Hi, everyone. Don't get up," he said as he hung the tie and his suit jacket on a wall hook.

"I'll make up your plate," Anne said.

"Thanks, sweetheart," he said, and then began to work his way around the table, sharing hugs and kisses and shaking outstretched hands.

When he sat down, the food was at his place, and next to it was a cut crystal tumbler holding four ice cubes and a healthy shot of Scotch. He picked up the glass. "It's so wonderful to have you all home. Let's make this a marvellous holiday."

Jack sat at one end of the table and his wife at the other. Several times during the meal she saw him staring at her, but every time she made eye contact, he lowered his head.

She thought something might be worrying him, although he wasn't displaying any obvious signs of concern.

Drinks were poured continually throughout dinner. Anne restricted herself to two martinis, but the others let loose, and no one more than Jack. Anne couldn't remember the last time she'd seen him drink so much.

The family never ate dessert, so when the last of the lasagna was consumed and the table had been cleared, Anne said, "Scrabble?"

"Of course," Brent said.

"I'll get the boards," Mark said.

Scrabble was an Anderson family tradition. When the children were young, it was Anne's way of helping the family bond, and Jack's way of breeding competitiveness. They played at least once a week until the children went off to university. Now Scrabble was reserved for holidays or whenever else the family managed to get together.

Three boards were laid on the kitchen table, and tiles were drawn to determine the pairings for the first round. Anne was the odd one out, which didn't bother her; she quite enjoyed flitting from contest to contest.

There was a strict time limit of thirty seconds per move and the length of a game was restricted to thirty minutes. When the first game ended, scores were announced, Anne replaced the low scorer, and tiles were redrawn. So it went for three hours, as the drinks continued to flow. Strangely, Anne never had a chance to play against Jack, and odder still, he had the lowest score in two of the rounds.

When the last game had ended, Anne and Allison carried the drink glasses to the dishwasher while Mark and Brent put away the boards.

"Is everything okay with Dad?" Allison asked quietly.

"I think so," Anne said. "Why do you ask?"

"He seemed very distracted. He's usually a demon at Scrabble, but tonight it felt like he didn't care if he won or lost."

"He's probably just tired. He left the house at six this morning, and you saw what time he got back."

"Still, it isn't like him."

"With retirement looming, I think he's becoming more conscious of his age and his capacity for work. When we started dating, I'd see him on Friday and Saturday nights and on Sunday mornings at church. The rest of the time he was working. When we were first married, and after you kids started coming along, he cut back some, but I remember having to insist that he spend weekends at home — even if he brought work with him — and I had to fight to get him to take two weeks off in the summer."

"How is he ever going to manage retirement?"

"Mark asked me the same question. I said Dad will do charitable work and join some boards, but the truth is I don't really know. He hasn't talked to me about it."

"Does he really have to pack it in?"

"When Bob Young was removed as president and CEO of Pilgrim, it was because the board of directors had passed a resolution limiting the time any one person could occupy either of those positions to twenty years," she said. "Your father initiated and promoted that resolution. When it passed, he assumed control of the company. Now it's come back to bite him in the ass — his words, not mine. He says it would be hypocritical of him not to play by the rules he used to force out Bob."

"That's Dad for you. Always doing the honourable thing."

"What are you two talking about?" a voice asked from behind.

They turned and saw Jack looking down at them, his eyes a bit glazed and his speech slightly slurred.

"We were talking about you," Anne said.

"Nothing nasty, I hope."

"How could you even think that's possible?" Allison said.

"From you two, I'd like to believe it's unlikely," he said, laughing, and then spoke directly to his wife. "I'm going to sit in the library for a while. There's a book I've been meaning to finish, and tonight seems like a good night for it."

"Which book?" she asked.

"*The Prince of Tides.*"

"That's my usual type of read, not yours. Whatever made you pick it up?"

"I don't really know, but I did, and now I intend to finish it, so don't wait up for me," he said.

"Don't worry about that. I'll be sleeping in a matter of minutes. Don't wake me."

"I won't. Goodnight. Sweet dreams," he said, and stepped forward to kiss each woman on the forehead.

Allison watched him pick up the bottle of Scotch from the sideboard and carry it and a clean glass into the library. "*Prince of Tides* is fiction, isn't it? He doesn't normally read fiction."

"He will read historical fiction, like Gore Vidal's, but this book is a departure. It's about a man and his twin sister trying to cope with a dysfunctional family. I have no idea what made your father start reading it—or why he thinks he has to finish it."

2

ANNE SLEPT WELL UNTIL she was awakened by the faint but persistent noise of Ainsley crying. From the moment her first child was born, she had been hypersensitive to baby noises. She could hear them through thick walls several rooms away, and even when she was outside the house and the baby inside. She couldn't explain why her hearing was so sensitive, and had never tried to. It was enough that everyone came to accept that it was Mother's special gift, so when she knocked on Brent and Maggie's bedroom door, Brent knew who it was and had the baby ready to hand over to her.

"Maggie has changed her. The formula bottle is in a saucepan on the stove. All you have to do is heat it," Brent said. "We'll be down shortly."

"No rush," Anne said, taking Ainsley.

It was just past six-thirty and the house was quiet. The winding staircase that led to the ground floor was heavily carpeted, and Anne's descent was silent except for the cooing of the baby. Compared to the action of the night before, the kitchen was eerily quiet. Anne turned on the stove and sat on one of the benches with the baby on her lap. A few minutes later she decided the formula was warm enough for Ainsley and started feeding her. Before she had finished, Maggie came into the kitchen.

"You could have stayed in bed," Anne said. "I have things under control."

"I know you do, but I can't seem to sleep in anymore."

Anne looked at the baby. "She has taken to the bottle very well."

"I felt so guilty when I weaned her."

"I've read that breast milk is perfect for the first few months, but after that there's nothing inferior about formula."

"I know, but I miss the bonding that breastfeeding gave us."

"There is that difference," Anne said. "Do you know that I never breastfed any of my children?"

"I do know, but it wasn't fashionable in those days."

"That isn't why. I'm afraid my reason was vanity," Anne said. "My best friend from high school, Mary Hughes, had three children before she was twenty-five and she breastfed them all. When I saw what a mess they'd made of her breasts, I decided it wasn't for me."

"Anne!"

"Sorry, Maggie. I wasn't suggesting that your breasts aren't still wonderful."

"Well, Brent doesn't complain about them."

"And that's all that matters."

Maggie smiled and stretched a hand towards Anne. "If he knew we were talking about this he'd be quite shocked."

"He's like his father in so many ways, and being prudish is one of them. If you asked Jack how he happens to have three children, he would act as if he had no idea how they were conceived."

"Oh my god, that is so Brent," Maggie said. "When we're in bed, he treats me as if every time is the first. He never takes me for granted, and I can't tell you how much I appreciate that. I have friends whose husbands treat them like they're being paid to perform tricks."

"Who's paid to perform tricks?" Brent said from the doorway.

"No one you'd know," Maggie said.

He walked into the kitchen and leaned over to kiss his mother. "Do you want me to make coffee?" he asked.

"Please."

By the time Brent had the coffee brewing, Ainsley had finished her bottle and was being burped.

"It's going to be a beautiful day. I'm looking forward to our walk," Brent said.

"I won't be joining you today. I have too much to do in the kitchen," Anne said.

"And I'll be helping your mother," Maggie said.

"I hope the others are more willing."

"They always are. I've never seen a family that likes

to hang around together as much as the Andersons," Maggie said.

"Maybe that's because we're such a small family," Anne said. "Jack and I are both only children of only children, so there have never been aunts, uncles, or cousins in the picture. And our parents are dead, so the people under this roof are the entirety of who we are."

"And we were raised to support and look after each other. The family comes first for all of us. There wasn't anything Mom or Dad wouldn't do for us, and we kids adopted that same attitude," Brent said.

"And of course we feel the same way about our children's partners," Anne said.

A beep from the coffee machine interrupted the conversation. "Can I pour for everyone?" Brent asked, and then walked to the counter without waiting for a reply.

Over the next couple of hours, the remainder of the family straggled into the kitchen, with Jack the last to arrive. Fresh coffee was made and then made again, eggs were boiled and poached, bacon and sausages fried, and most of a loaf of bread toasted. At nine o'clock, as the last of the breakfast dishes were being put in the dishwasher, Anne said, "Okay, it's time for you all to leave. Maggie and I need the kitchen to ourselves. We have a turkey that will take close to four hours to cook, and we need to get it ready for the oven."

"Time for a walk," Brent said. "It's so nice outside I don't think we'll need jackets. Sweaters should do."

"This is when I miss Buffy," Allison said to her mother. "I'll never understand why you didn't get another dog after she died."

"She was always your dog. Neither your father nor I have the patience to look after one on our own," Anne said.

As the family gathered near the front door, Jack hung back in the kitchen. "Aren't you going with the children?" Anne asked.

"I think I'm going to pass," he said. "I went to bed rather late last night and didn't sleep well."

"Are you feeling all right?"

"I'm just a bit tired."

"The fresh air might do you some good."

"I think I'd rather sit in the den and finish that book."

"The children will be disappointed."

"I'll explain it to them," Jack said, and went over to the front door.

From the kitchen Anne could hear him tell the children he wasn't going with them. She frowned when she heard their disappointed reactions. It wasn't like Jack not to go on the walk. She hoped he wouldn't decline to play in the touch football game on the front lawn that typically followed it.

As Jack came back through the kitchen on his way to the den, Anne saw Maggie eyeing him with concern. After he had closed the den door behind him, Anne said to her, "There's no need to worry. If there's something wrong I'm sure he'd tell us."

"Brent thinks that as retirement gets closer, the reality

of it is beginning to weigh on Jack," Maggie said.

"Brent could be right," Anne said. "Jack has made some comments recently that seem out of character. For example, Pilgrim had its annual meeting at the end of September. He mentioned three or four times that it was his last one and he wanted it to be first-rate. Most years I had no idea the meeting was even happening."

"Did the company do anything special for him at the meeting?"

"I don't know," Anne said. "He's never wanted me to attend company functions. It's his other life, and I'm not part of it. I don't mind, though. I've always had enough on my plate with the children and the house."

"I'm sure they'll do something to honour him. Jack Anderson *is* Pilgrim."

"I hope so. He certainly deserves it," Anne said. "Now, how about Brent? Does he include you in his company's events?"

"He does ask me, but most often I choose not to go."

"Can I give you some advice?" Anne asked.

"Sure."

"You should start going. What you don't want is for him to stop asking."

"Maybe when the baby is a bit older."

"Don't wait that long. Babies have a way of never becoming quite old enough. Before you know it, they're teenagers and you have an entirely new set of challenges to worry about."

"I'll keep that in mind," Maggie said, laughing.

The two women worked side by side for the next few hours until the turkey was stuffed and in the oven and the yams, potatoes, green beans, cranberry sauce, and a small ham were prepped and sitting on the counter. They were at the kitchen table enjoying a fresh cup of coffee when the front door opened.

"We're back," Mark shouted, and then walked into the kitchen. "Time for football."

"How far did you walk?" Anne asked.

"How far is it from here to the town centre?"

"Almost three miles."

"Then that's how far we went. We stopped for a leisurely coffee at a bistro and then walked back. It took us twice as long to get home. I'd forgotten how much of the walk from town is uphill."

"It is a serious walk," Anne said. "I do it three times a week."

"Which means you're fit enough to play football."

"I'm fit enough to play *at* football," she said. "After all these years I still don't know how to catch the darn thing."

"That puts you in good company — with Allison and Maggie," Mark said.

"Don't be such a male chauvinist," Maggie said.

"We'll move you from team to team so things will be even. C'mon, everyone else is waiting on the lawn," Mark said. Then he paused. "Where's Dad?"

"He's in the den. I'll get him," Anne said.

She went to the closed door, knocked, and then opened it. Jack sat in his red leather club chair with his feet on an ottoman. His head rested against the back of the chair, turned to one side, and his eyes were closed. *The Prince of Tides* lay open on his lap.

Anne nudged his arm. "Jack, the kids are back from their walk and they're ready to play football."

Jack shook his head, and for a second she thought he was going to refuse to join them. Then he said, "Give me a minute. I need to go to the bathroom and then I'll be right there."

Anne joined the rest of the family on the lawn. Jack arrived a few minutes later, just in time to be selected by Brent for his team. Mark was the other team captain. There were times when it bothered Anne to see how competitive her children were, but this wasn't one of them. Everyone gave it their full effort, of course, or they wouldn't have been Andersons, but the ragging was good-natured and the scorekeeping was haphazard.

The game went on for more than an hour, until Anne called for an end. "I've got vegetables that need my attention, and I want to see all of you at the table dressed for the occasion."

When they were younger, the children had often complained about the dress code that Anne imposed on Thanksgiving and Christmas dinners. Suits and ties were compulsory for the men, and the women were expected to wear a fashionable dress or skirt and blouse. The complaining had stopped after they all left home. Coming back meant a return to the familiar, and getting dressed up for Thanksgiving dinner was as much a part of family tradition as the turkey stuffed with oysters and sausage and their game of touch football.

The children trooped into the house, debating among themselves who would have first crack at the showers. Anne and Maggie headed for the kitchen. Jack stayed outside with Jonathan, the two of them sitting side by side on the stone stairs.

The boy looked up at his grandfather. "Mommy says I can play football next year," he said.

"I'd like that."

"And Mommy said that you lost your job, so you'll visit us more. I would like *that*."

"I haven't exactly lost my job, but I will have more time on my hands. And I do like California, when it isn't too hot."

Jonathan leaned against his grandfather, and Jack slipped his arm around the boy's shoulders. Their conversation died, but the two of them were content to sit quietly, absorbing the beautiful autumn day, until the front door opened and Anne appeared. "You two need to come inside and get ready," she said.

It was three o'clock when the family took their seats around the Regency oak table in the dining room. Jack had carved the turkey and ham in the kitchen, and the meats lay under sheets of aluminum foil in the middle of the table. Wine bottles were passed and glasses filled. Then all eyes turned to Jack.

He lowered his head. "Lord, we thank you for this bounty we are about to receive. We thank you for keeping our family healthy and for bringing us together. We ask for your blessing in the year to come. Please keep everyone well and let all our dreams be realized. Amen."

After a chorus of amens, Allison raised her glass. "On behalf of all of us, a big thanks to Mom and Dad. May the coming year be wonderful, and may all the years that follow be as happy and fruitful as the years that have gone before."

"Thank you, sweetheart," Anne said, and then pointed at the food. "Now, I want everyone to have at least two helpings."

Both wine and gravy flowed freely until the mounds of green beans, mashed potatoes and yams, and trays of turkey and ham were decimated. The children talked easily among themselves, Brent quizzing Tony about the economic ins and outs of the film business, Tony pressing Mark for details about how traders operated, and Maggie asking Allison for gossip about the movie stars she'd met.

Anne sat back listening, fascinated by her children's exploits. She looked at Jack, expecting him to be as engaged as she was. Instead he sat stone-faced, as if he had no interest in the table banter. He had been quiet during the meal, but this was different, and Anne wasn't the only person to notice.

"Mom, is Dad okay?" Allison, who was sitting next to her mother, whispered.

Anne nodded to indicate she'd heard the question and then turned to her husband. "Jack, is everything all right? You seem distracted. Is something bothering you?"

He looked at her. "As a matter of fact," he said sombrely, "something is bothering me."

The table became quiet, and every eye turned to him.

"You're scaring me," Anne said. "Are you ill?"

"No, I'm not ill. Not in body anyway."

"Jack, please," Anne said. "What is going on?"

"I have something I need to say to the entire family," he said.

"You're not going to retire, right?" Mark said. "I didn't think you would."

"Please, don't interrupt," Anne said. "Let Daddy speak."

"What I have to say is simple enough," Jack said. "I have a sister."

3

ANNE'S MOUTH FLEW OPEN. "What?"

No one else spoke, but astonished glances were exchanged as Jack's declaration began to sink in.

"More properly, I guess I should say I've always known that I had one," Jack continued. "But I didn't know until yesterday that she's still alive."

"But you're an only child," Anne declared.

"I was raised as one, and I told you I was one, but the truth is I'm not."

"Dad, are you trying to tell us that Grandpa or Grandma had a child on the side?" Allison asked.

"Goodness me, no, nothing like that."

"Then how can you have a sister?" Allison said.

"It's a long and complicated story," Jack said, looking at Anne, who sat in stunned silence.

"Are you going to tell it?" Allison asked.

"I think I've already upset your mother. I'm not sure I should continue."

"Well, you can't leave it like that," Anne said.

"If you would rather you and I talk first, I'm sure the children won't mind," he said.

"I wish you'd thought of that before you made your announcement," she said, the hurt obvious in her voice.

"I'm sorry. I've been thinking about this for days, and I wasn't sure until a few minutes ago that I could actually go through with it," he said. "Forgive me, Anne."

She nodded. "Well, what's done is done, and I'm sure the children are as curious as I am. It isn't fair to make them wait."

"Okay, but I'm not going to pretend this is easy for me," Jack said. "Mark, could you pour me a stiff whisky, please?"

Mark nodded and went to the buffet where the liquor was kept, returning with a glass of Scotch. Jack took a large sip. "I've always hated the term 'liquid courage,' but this time it seems appropriate," he said. "Now, where was I?"

"You just finished telling us you have a sister, which, as Mom has correctly pointed out, has left us all rather confused and curious," Allison said.

"Grandpa and Grandma Anderson weren't my birth parents," Jack said. He saw his wife's face collapse in disbelief. "I'm sorry. Maybe I really should stop."

"You're in too deep for that," Allison said.

Jack shook his head. "With all of us together, I thought

this would be the best time to talk about this. I'm not sure now that I made the right decision."

"I agree with Allison. You have to tell us the rest of the story," Brent said. "Mom, are you in agreement with that?"

Anne hesitated and then looked at her husband. "I want you to finish what you've started."

"You don't sound particularly convinced," Jack said.

"What I am is unhappy that my husband has kept this secret from me all these years."

"You're leaping to a conclusion, Mom. This is something Dad may have just learned himself. I know that a lot of information about their birth families is kept secret from children who are adopted when they're young," Allison said. "Dad, is this something you've just found out?"

"No, I've always known. I wasn't a baby when it happened," Jack said.

"Then why didn't you tell me?" Anne said.

"Because I preferred to believe that I wasn't adopted, that Martin and Colleen were my real parents. They wanted to believe the same thing, so we believed it together," he said. "Right from the moment I was adopted, Colleen loved me and called me her own, and I was only too happy to be hers. We pretended for so long that I was born to her that it became our reality. She and Martin never saw any harm in it, and neither did I. So why should I talk about my early life when I had convinced myself it never happened?"

"How old were you when they adopted you?" Brent asked.

"Six."

"My god. Did you know your birth parents?"

Jack nodded. "Their names were Andrew and Jessie McPherson. They lived in Glasgow, Scotland. I think he was a labourer of some kind."

"You remember that?" Brent asked.

"It isn't so much."

"Life must have been very difficult for them to have put you up for adoption," Maggie said.

"They didn't put me up for adoption. They . . . discarded me."

"I don't understand," Maggie said.

"More Scotch, please," Jack said to Mark, holding up his glass. "You might as well leave the bottle on the table."

"People can't just get rid of children," Maggie said.

"Maybe not in Massachusetts, but in Glasgow in 1934 it was simply enough done," Jack said. "My mother took me and my sister to a matinee at a movie theatre, left at intermission to take my sister to the bathroom, and never returned. I was told that the authorities contacted my father later that night to tell him what had happened and where I was. He said they could keep me. He didn't want me."

A silence fell over the table. Everyone looked awkwardly at each other, unsure about how to react. Finally Maggie said, "How terrible."

"That's one word for it," Mark added.

"And you were only six?" Brent said.

"Yes."

"But you remember all that?" Allison asked.

"How could he forget it?" Brent said.

"Well, I did try to forget it, for many years. The most painful part of what I've been going through these past few months is that once I decided that I wanted to remember, those are the memories that came back to me most vividly."

"But how did you get from Scotland to Watertown?"

"When my father refused to claim me, I was taken in by a Catholic charity. Glasgow was mainly Protestant, so there wasn't a big demand for adopting Catholic children, especially six-year-old boys. Luckily, one of the nuns with the charity was from Boston, and even more fortunately, she had a younger brother named Martin Anderson who was looking to adopt a child."

"Dad, do you know how weird all this sounds?" Mark said.

"I know it isn't what you've been raised to believe."

Allison left her chair and walked to the head of the table. She stood behind her father and wrapped her arms around him, pressing her cheek against his. "How awful those memories must be for you."

"I'm trying not to be overly dramatic, and I don't want you to be. At the end of the day, I was as loved as any child could be, and I had a wonderfully supportive upbringing."

"How can you call being abandoned as a small child anything other than dramatic?" Allison said.

"I think 'cruel' and 'heartless' are better descriptions," Maggie said, her voice catching and tears welling in her eyes.

"Whatever you call it doesn't really matter to me," Jack said. "I'd rather deal with the present than the past."

"And the present is this sister you've uncovered," Anne said.

"It is."

"Do you know where she is?" asked Anne.

"According to the U.K. National Health Service, she's living in a town called Irvine on the west coast of Scotland."

"Dad, what prompted you to look for her in the first place?" Mark asked.

Jack paused, sipped his whisky, and said, "I guess she was always lurking in the back of my mind. Not often, but every now and then I'd get a flash of memory and I'd wonder what became of her, and my blood parents. Then, about six months ago our legal department brought in a new crop of interns, and among them was a young woman named Moira. That was my sister's name. I didn't see Moira the lawyer very often, but whenever I did it would trigger thoughts of my sister.

"I also think my upcoming retirement was a factor. I'm not, as you know, given to much sentimentality, but as I began to contemplate leaving Pilgrim, I found myself reliving the old days — when I first joined the company, my climb up the corporate ladder, and my years as CEO. As I thought about that past, the other past intruded. It began to feel like unfinished business."

"When did you start this search?" Mark asked.

"About two months ago. I had thought about hiring a private detective, but Larry Andrews, our comptroller, mentioned at a meeting—completely by coincidence—that he was constructing his family tree and that most of it was Scottish. I asked how he was going about it. He said the U.K. government has terrific records and mentioned that the health services were particularly helpful. So I wrote a letter to the U.K. National Health Service office in Glasgow explaining who I was and where and when I was born. I told them about my relationship to Andrew, Jessie, and Moira McPherson and asked if they could provide information on any of them. About three weeks later I got a reply saying they had forwarded my request to an office in London. A few days ago I got a letter from London."

"Telling you that Moira is alive and living in Irvine?" Mark said.

"Yes. They even provided an address. But there was nothing on Andrew or Jessie. I assume they're dead."

"Good riddance to them," Allison said.

"Allie!" Anne snapped.

"After what they did to Dad, how else am I supposed to feel?"

"What do you know about this Moira?" Maggie asked.

"Only that she lives in Irvine."

"Does she have children?"

"I have no idea. I don't know if she married or became a nun. I know absolutely nothing about her except the fact that the health service says she's alive."

"What are you going to do now that you know where she is?" Mark asked.

"I'm not sure. That partially depends on your mother," Jack said, looking at Anne. "I think I would like to contact Moira, and if she's agreeable I might visit her, but I would like your mom to be okay with it all."

"Why?" Anne asked.

"We're a team. I know I should have told you about this sooner, and I'm sorry I didn't, but now that I have, I'd like you to be part of this with me."

"No, I meant why would you want to see her," Anne said.

"Ah," Jack said. He fell into a silence that lasted for perhaps a minute but seemed much longer.

"Dad, Mom asked you a question that interests all of us," Allison said, finally breaking the quiet.

Jack looked around the table, but his eyes seemed to be wandering, not focusing on anyone. "I guess you could say I want to know how, and I want to know why."

"What are you trying to say?" Anne asked.

"I want to know how a mother could abandon one child and save another," he said. "I want to know why she left my father, her husband. I want to know what happened in the rest of her life, and if she ever thought of me again."

"Do you think this Moira will be able to answer those questions?" Anne asked.

"Perhaps."

"What if Moira doesn't want to see you?" Allison asked.

"Then I guess I'll never get my answers," he said.

4

THE DAYS FOLLOWING JACK'S disclosure were emotional. While the family tried to be supportive, there was some tension as everyone tried to absorb the fact that Jack Anderson — as a husband and then as a father — had concealed such a large truth from them. Anne was the most affected, and when she discussed it with her children in Jack's absence, she was subject to moods that swung from empathy to anger.

On the Sunday following Thanksgiving, Jack was in town with Jonathan. Anne was sitting with Maggie, Brent, Allison, and Tony at the kitchen table when the discussion turned again to Jack's admission.

"Will you go to Scotland with him to meet the sister?" Allison asked her mother.

"Before I make that decision, he has to decide if he's going himself," Anne said. "He has been drafting a letter to her, but he's rewritten it at least four times."

"Why doesn't he just phone?" Allison said.

"He doesn't have her number, and he suspects she might not have a phone."

"Okay, but what if he sends it and she tells him to get on the first plane to Scotland? Will you go with him?"

"I don't know," Anne said, and then added quickly, "Part of me wants to because I think he could use the support, but another part of me feels betrayed—as if I'd just discovered he's been having an affair all these years, and now he wants me to meet the mistress."

"That's a ridiculous comparison," Maggie said.

Four surprised faces turned in her direction.

"I don't mean to be rude, but for the last three days I've listened to everyone bemoaning the fact that Jack kept a secret from the family, and I have to say I think we've got it all backwards," Maggie said. "Instead of focusing on the impact on us, we should be asking why he kept it buried for so long, and thinking about the pain he's going through now that he's finally confronting what happened to him."

"What would you have me do?" Anne asked.

"I'd like you to be the kind and supportive woman I've always known," Maggie said. "Help him write the letter. And if his sister responds positively, get on a plane with him and go see her."

"It's just been such a shock," Anne said.

"Imagine the shock of being abandoned by your mother at the age of six," Maggie said.

"Maggie is right," Allison said. "I don't know how Dad survived that and became the man he is."

Anne wiped a tear from her eye. "I know he must have been in pain. I mean, I know he told us he didn't think about it, but how is that even possible? My only regret—no, my only wish is that he had told me sooner."

"But he didn't—maybe because he couldn't," Maggie said. "Now he has, and what he needs is for us to rally to his support. And he needs no one more than you, Anne."

Maggie's words sank in. That night, after the children had left, Anne went to the den, where Jack was still struggling through *The Prince of Tides*.

"I know you've been working on a letter to your sister. Can I help you with it?" she said.

"I'd like that," he replied.

The next day the letter was sent, and for the next three weeks Anne haunted the mailbox until they received a reply. It was terse and rather suspicious in tone and did not include the phone number Jack had requested.

"I think you were right about her not having a phone," Anne said.

"Maybe I was," Jack said, disappointment in his voice. He had mixed expectations when the response came, but he hadn't anticipated what he was reading.

Dear Mr. Anderson
I am in receipt of your letter dated November 30 from Boston, U.S.A.

You were right to think the news it contained would come as a surprise to me. I did have a brother named Jack, but this is the first I've heard that he went to America. If you are my brother, and I have no reason to doubt you or your explanation for the family name change, then I'm pleased to know that you are alive and well.

I am not sure what good can come from us meeting, but if you did come to Scotland, I would be willing to sit with you.

Yours sincerely,

Moira McPherson

Jack wrote back to say that he indeed planned to visit Scotland and asked which dates would be best for her to see him. He also asked if she could tell him what had become of their mother and father. Moira replied in early January.

I hate to think you would be coming all that way just to see me. But Irvine is in the heart of Robert Burns country, and there are many historic sites within an easy car ride. Glasgow itself is only thirty minutes away. As for me, I don't stray far from the house. I'm in most days. I used to work at the woollen mill but had to give it up when my emphysema became too bad.

The weather is usually fierce in January and February, so if you want to come I would suggest from March on. I wouldn't come any sooner.

With regard to your question about our parents, I think you should know that my mother has been dead for many years now. I have no idea what became of him, although given how much he used to drink, I'd be surprised if he was still alive.

Yours sincerely,

Moira McPherson

"That's rather a cold letter," Anne said after she read it. "And that remark about 'my mother' — she could at least have acknowledged that she was your mother as well."

"Reading between the lines, it seems to me that she's not a woman who's been very successful in life," Jack said. "She's still using the name McPherson, so I'm assuming she's never been married. Her manner could simply be that of a shy and lonely woman."

"Are you still intent on going to Scotland?"

"Will you come with me?"

"Of course, but I have to tell you I'm glad your sister mentioned Robert Burns and those historic sites. If she fails you, we'll at least have those to fall back on."

"What do you think about her idea of going in March? Personally I don't care about the weather, and I'd rather not wait that long," he said. "Irvine is only a few miles from Prestwick Airport, and there are direct flights from Logan to Prestwick two or three times a week, year-round."

"She might have another reason for suggesting March," Anne said. "Maybe, for example, she isn't ready to see you yet. I think we should respect her wishes, don't you?"

"I guess so, though I really don't like having to put this off," he said.

Anne picked up a calendar from his desk and turned to March. "Easter is the last weekend in March, and we have nothing to keep us here before that. Why don't you ask your assistant to book us flights to Prestwick in the first week of the month."

"Okay, but since the trip is personal, I'd rather ask the local travel agent to make the reservations. How long do you want to stay?"

"There's no point in travelling all that way for less than a week," Anne said.

"I'll look after it tomorrow," he said.

5

Ayrshire, Scotland
March 1989

THREE WEEKS BEFORE EASTER, after an overnight flight, Jack and Anne landed at Prestwick International Airport, which was about ten miles south of Irvine. Jack picked up their rental car at the airport and drove to the Marine Hotel in Troon, about three miles to the north. They had arranged to see Moira the following day; Jack's immediate plan was for them to get caught up on sleep and become acclimatized to the surroundings. They checked in, ate a big breakfast, went to their suite, and promptly fell asleep.

It was early afternoon when Jack woke. He opened the curtains on a grey, rainy day. The hotel overlooked the Royal Troon Golf Club, one of the rotating venues for the British Open. From his window he could see golfers scurrying along a fairway with umbrellas in front of their faces to deflect the wind and rain. He had heard that Scots golfed in all weathers, but he wasn't sure that spoke well of them.

He roused Anne. "We should do something active," he said. "If we hang around we'll just want to sleep, and then we'll be up all night and jet-lagged for the next week."

While Anne showered, Jack called the front desk to ask about local Burns sites. He was told they were nearly all in and around the town of Ayr, about eleven miles to the south, and that a local tour bus was scheduled to make a pickup at the hotel at three. Jack booked two places on the bus.

They didn't get back to the hotel until six, after three hours of trying to stay dry at the Burns Monument, the Robbie Burns Cottage, the Robert Burns Museum, the Alloway Auld Kirk, and the Brig o' Doon, a narrow cobbled footbridge that Burns had immortalized in his poem "Tam o' Shanter." They towelled dry their hair, changed clothes, and then went downstairs for dinner.

As soon as they sat down in the dining room they ordered a martini for Anne and a Scotch for Jack.

"You know when I was at UMass I had to put up with and absorb way more Emily Dickinson than seems humane, but I've never seen a poet idolized as much as Robert Burns," Anne said.

"Is that a criticism?"

"Not at all. People should love poetry and their poets."

"Then what are you trying to say?"

"We're not in Wellesley anymore."

Jack raised an eyebrow.

"What I mean is that this is a different country and a

different culture. They may speak English—albeit with an accent—but they aren't us."

The waiter arrived with the drinks and the conversation died. They toasted each other's health and then sipped appreciatively as they looked at the menu.

"Roast beef for me, I think," Jack said.

"There's a surprise."

"And for you?"

"Dover sole."

"Also a surprise."

"The real surprise," Anne said carefully, "is that we haven't discussed your sister since we landed."

"I've been trying not to think about her."

"Why is that?"

"Maybe I'm afraid she's changed her mind and won't invite me in when I show up on her doorstep."

"Jack, you've read her letters. I'd be shocked if she didn't. But I also wouldn't have any expectations that she'll be particularly welcoming."

"Is there a reason why you can't be more positive about this?" he asked abruptly.

Anne heard the anxiety in his voice and sensed she might have hit a nerve. "I'm sorry. All I'm trying to say is that the woman might not have all the answers."

"I'm prepared for that."

"Good. Then you won't be disappointed, no matter how it turns out."

Jack started to respond but stopped when the waiter

reappeared. They ordered the beef and sole and another round of drinks. "I don't think I want to discuss my sister anymore tonight," he said when the waiter had left. "Neither of us can predict what's going to happen tomorrow, so it's pointless to speculate."

"Jack, all I want is for you to be satisfied, to get some kind of closure," Anne said, reaching for his hand. "Although I know you'll never admit it, I think the past few months have been difficult for you. Too often I've seen you staring off into space as if you were somewhere else. That isn't like you."

"I have been somewhere else."

"Where?"

"I've been sitting in a movie house," he said.

"What?"

"I've been sitting by myself in a movie house, waiting for my mother to come back."

6

THE NEXT MORNING JACK woke at five after a sleepless night. Anne hadn't shared his restlessness and was still gently snoring when he closed the bedroom door behind him and went into the sitting room. He opened his briefcase and took out the work he'd brought with him. As he leafed through it, he phoned his assistant's line in Boston to leave a succession of messages and instructions. There was a five-hour time difference between Troon and Boston, so it was midnight there.

He worked steadily until just past seven, when Anne appeared in the doorway. "Have you ordered coffee yet?" she asked.

"There's no room service until seven," he said, checking his watch. "I can order it now."

At eight-thirty they made their way downstairs for breakfast. Jack stopped at the concierge's desk to pick up a local map and a guide to Ayrshire. Pam, his personal assistant at Pilgrim, had already given him very specific driving instructions from the Marine Hotel to Moira's Bank Street address, but Jack wanted a better feel for the entire area. He perused the map and the guide over a breakfast of Ayrshire bacon, potato scones, and fried eggs. He had declined the blood pudding, even though he was told it was the perfect accompaniment to the rest of his meal.

"It says here that on a clear day we should be able to see the Isle of Arran across the Firth of Clyde," Jack said, looking out a rain-streaked window at the misty Royal Troon golf course.

"If we have time and the weather is decent, that might be a nice side trip, assuming there's a ferry to take us across," Anne said.

"Better still, Kilmarnock is only five or six miles east of Irvine, and it's the home of Johnnie Walker whisky. The guide recommends a tour of the distillery."

After you see your sister, the distillery might be necessary, Anne thought.

It had stopped raining when they left the hotel, but it was cold and blustery. Anne wore a raincoat over a thick angora sweater and wool slacks. Jack had on a long-sleeved polo shirt, jeans, a blue blazer, and a Boston Red Sox cap. Anne saw several women in the lobby eyeing him as they walked by. If anything ever happened to her, she was sure there would be a lineup of women at the door.

"Here are the directions I got from Pam," he said, handing her a slip of paper as they got into their Ford Escort. "You're in charge of navigating."

The roads were well signed and the directions precise. The Andersons found themselves in the centre of the old town of Irvine within twenty minutes of leaving the hotel. Jack drove along the High Street, then turned onto Bank. Moira lived in the middle of a row of rather grim-looking houses, their doors set into walls of grey stone with windows on either side. Some of the doors had been painted bright colours and some of the windows had lace curtains, but Jack couldn't help but think of the houses as institutional. Moira's door was a dull brown, and instead of curtains there were half-drawn blinds.

Jack parked on the street directly in front of Moira's house. As he got out of the car he thought he saw someone moving behind one of the blinds.

Anne joined him on the sidewalk. "Are you ready?" she asked.

"As ready as I'll ever be."

They walked up to the house. He knocked and took two steps back. When the door opened, he felt immediate disappointment.

The woman was at least a foot shorter than his six feet four inches, and even wearing a baggy sweater over an ankle-length dress, she looked skeletal. Her hair was greyish white and hung limply around a face that was all jutting bones, except for the washed-out blue eyes.

"Hello, you must be Jack," she said, exposing stained yellow teeth.

He looked at her fingers and saw dark nicotine stains. "I am, and you must be Moira."

"I am."

"This is my wife, Anne," he said.

"Come inside," Moira said, without a shred of enthusiasm and not offering either of them her hand, let alone anything as intimate as a hug.

They walked into a tiny vestibule furnished only with a four-pronged wooden coat rack. "You can put your coats there if you like," Moira said.

Anne took off her raincoat and hung it on the rack. Jack put his cap next to it.

"We'll go into the sitting room. I've put the heat on," Moira said.

They followed her into a small room with a window that looked onto the street. A sofa and two easy chairs were grouped around a coffee table holding a teapot, three cups and saucers, a sugar bowl, and a small milk jar. A small television sat on an end table in the corner. Behind the sofa was a large, colourful print of what looked like the charge of the Light Brigade.

Moira closed the door behind them. "I hope you don't mind me closing the door, but this radiator is the only heat I have in the house."

"I don't mind at all," Jack said. "Where would you like us to sit?"

"Wherever you wish. I'll sit in this chair," Moira said, slipping into the easy chair closest to the window.

Jack sat down on the sofa and Anne sat next to him.

"Would you like a cup of tea?" Moira asked. "It won't take long to boil some water."

Jack shook his head while Anne said, "No, but thank you all the same. We drank too many cups of coffee this morning."

Moira nodded. "How was your journey?" she asked in a matter-of-fact manner.

"Long and tiring. It might take us a few days to get over the jet lag," Jack said.

"I've never been on an aeroplane," Moira said. "It must be exciting."

"After a while it isn't much different than getting into a car," he said.

"I wouldn't know," she said, turning her head and looking out the window.

"I want to thank you for agreeing to see me," he said.

"How could I say no?"

"So you've accepted the fact that I'm your brother?"

"Aye. Why would anyone invent a story like that?"

"It isn't a story. It happened. I remember it quite clearly."

"Actually, so do I. It took a wee while, but eventually it came back to me."

"That's good to know," said Jack.

"Why?"

"Because maybe you can explain to me why she did it."

Moira blinked. Her fingers gripped the hem of her sweater and she began to rub it between them. She looked at Anne. "You're very blonde. Is the colour real?"

"It is. My family is Estonian and we're all blonde."

"Estonian. Is that Christian?"

"Very Christian. My father was a Lutheran minister."

"I'm Presbyterian."

"Which means that we're both Protestants. For some reason Jack ended up as a Catholic."

"So he's a Celtic supporter."

"I beg your pardon?" Anne said. "I don't understand what you mean."

"All the Catholics in Scotland support Glasgow Celtic. The Protestants support the Glasgow Rangers."

"I don't support either of them," Jack said.

"You don't like footie?"

"No."

"When I worked at the knitting mill, I supported Irvine Meadow. Their grounds were only a few hundred yards from the mill, and after working on a Saturday morning, all the girls from the mill would go there to cheer on the lads. One of the girls married a Meadow player, but at least three others got pregnant and there weren't any marriages."

Jack sat forward on the sofa, his elbows on his knees. "That's all very interesting, Moira, but it doesn't answer my question."

"Which question is that?"

"Why did my mother — our mother — leave me in the movie house?"

Moira looked at Anne. "This is upsetting. All very upsetting."

"I can understand that it is for you, but it's also upsetting for Jack. He's simply looking for an explanation of something he can't understand," Anne said.

"Why not?" she said.

"What do you mean?" asked Anne.

"Why can't he understand? He lived in the house. He had eyes and ears."

"And what was Jack supposed to have seen and heard?"

"The beltings."

"Your father beat your mother?"

"Every Saturday night, like clockwork. He'd come home drunk, and it didn't matter if she was asleep or hiding, he'd find her and take the strap to her," Moira said. She looked at Jack. "Don't tell me you don't remember. He'd wake us sometimes and make us watch."

Jack shook his head. "I don't remember anything like that. In fact, I remember virtually nothing about my life here or the people in it before the day at the movie house. I can recall names but not faces, and certainly not events like the kind you're describing."

Moira turned back towards the window, her jaw set firmly, the blue veins in her forehead pulsing. The room became uncomfortably silent.

Anne saw the confusion on her husband's face and

the determination on Moira's. "Are you saying that your mother left your father because he beat her?" she asked.

"Aye, of course she did. And who could blame her?"

"I couldn't," Anne said. "But when she left, why didn't she take Jack with her as well?"

"She didn't want our father chasing her. He loved Jack. She was afraid that if she took Jack, he'd come looking for him. She thought if she left Jack with him, he'd leave us alone."

"How do you know that?" Anne asked.

"I remember it because after we left the cinema I asked her where Jack was, and that was what she said. She repeated it over and over, and for days after that she kept going back to it. I had put it out of my mind until I got Jack's letter, and then it all started to come back to me."

"Except our father didn't want me. I was immediately put into an orphanage," Jack said. "In fact, I never saw him again."

"I didn't know that."

"Did our mother?"

"She never discussed that kind of thing with me," Moira said. "You know, maybe the fact that he didn't want you was a good thing."

"What do you mean?" Jack asked.

"With Mum gone, he might have started belting you," Moira said. She offered the slightest of smiles. "It seems to have worked out well enough for you. You seem to have made a very good life for yourself in America. If you had stayed here, who knows where you would have ended up."

"But didn't she care? Didn't she care enough to find out what had happened to me?"

"She was gone from him. I think that's all she cared about. You were part of the life she left behind."

"Was she really that unfeeling?" Anne asked.

"She was a hard woman, but then, she'd had a hard life," Moira said.

"And how has your life been?"

"I'm not one to complain."

"How did you end up in Irvine?" Jack asked.

"I left home when I was fifteen and rented a room in a small house owned by a widow lady in the Gorbals. When they tore down that part of the Gorbals, I had to move. A friend told me there was work to be had in Irvine at a knitting mill. I came here for a visit, liked it, and decided to stay after I got a job at the mill. In Glasgow after I left home, I'd been a dishwasher, a scullery worker, in various restaurants. It was nice to get my hands out of hot, greasy water."

"Where did our mother go? Did she stay in Glasgow?"

"She met a new man a few years after leaving our father. They lived in the Gorbals until the year I moved out of the house. Later he bought a place in Govan, on the other side of Glasgow."

"Did you stay in touch with her?" Anne asked.

"We weren't close."

"But you stayed in touch?"

"I visited her now and then in Glasgow, and she came here two or three times. She wasn't what you would call maternal, at least not with me."

"And even less so with Jack," Anne said.

"Like I said, she'd had a hard life," Moira said, looking across at Jack. "It's easy to find fault in her, even for me, and I'm a Christian woman. But in the end I think of her as a poor wee woman trying to survive as best she could."

"How did she die?" Jack asked.

"Cancer. She was a smoker."

"Was she buried?"

"She has her own grave with a fine headstone in the grounds behind St. Andrew's Church in Govan."

"Where is Govan?"

"On the outskirts of Glasgow, south of the Clyde and not far from the Gorbals."

"And our father?'

"Why would I know anything about him?"

"The National Health Service has no current records for him, which implies that he's dead."

"I hope that's right," she said.

"You hate him that much?"

"After what he did to our mother, how else could I feel? I know you probably feel the same way about her. Don't blame me if I don't."

"Moira, I don't blame you for anything. You were nine years old when all this happened."

"We were both wee, and neither of us had any idea

what kind of life the grownups in our lives were leading."

"That's true," Jack said. He noticed that Moira had let go of the hem of her sweater and seemed slightly more at ease. "It's also one of the reasons I came to Scotland, and why I'm talking to you. I thought I might find out about their lives."

"I've told you all I know. I hadn't thought about either of them in years, until you wrote to me. I have my own life to worry about."

"And how is your life?" Anne asked. "I mean, are things all right for you?"

"There's a library down the street and I have the telly. Some friends from the mill drop in now and then."

Jack looked at Moira and felt a twinge of pity. *What a wreck of a woman,* he thought. *But the circumstances of her life have nothing to do with me.* Their plan, if things went well, had been to ask Moira to join them for lunch. Now all he wanted to do was get out of her house. He stood up. "Well, we've taken up enough of your time. I think we should get going now."

Anne glanced at him, quickly recognized his mood, and got to her feet.

Moira nodded and struggled to rise. "I'll walk you to the door," she said.

"Don't bother," Jack said.

He and Anne left the room. Moira followed, then stood back and watched as Anne put on her raincoat. Jack reached for the doorknob.

"I suppose you're off to see the others," Moira said.

"The others?" Jack asked, his hand freezing.

"Georgina and Harry."

"Georgina and Harry?"

Moira searched his face as if she didn't believe him. "You don't know?"

"I don't know what?"

"Our mother was pregnant when she left our father," Moira said. "Georgina and Harry are the twins she had."

7

THEY TRAILED MOIRA BACK into the sitting room. Anne stopped at the door and squeezed Jack's hand. "I know this is a shock, but it will be all right," she said.

"Goddamn it," he whispered. "Why did she wait until we were at the door to spring that on us?"

"Stay calm. I know you're agitated, but it won't serve any purpose."

They took the seats they'd left only a few minutes before, but the mood in the room had shifted. "Why did you wait to tell me about Georgina and Harry?" Jack demanded.

Moira seemed flustered and looked to Anne as if asking for help.

"Obviously Moira thought you knew about them," Anne said to Jack. "Was there any mention of other children when you contacted the health service?"

"Nothing."

Anne smiled at Moira. "I'm sure you can understand

why Jack is so taken aback. He thought he was coming here to meet a long-lost sister, and now he's just found out that he's got a brother and a second sister."

"How was I to know that he didn't know?"

"Exactly. How could you know." Anne said. "Tell me, Moira, do Georgina and Harry use the family name McPherson?"

"No, they were raised as Montgomerys, and Georgina's married name is Malcolm."

"That explains it, then," Anne said to Jack. She turned back to Moira. "Was Montgomery your mother's maiden name?"

"No, she took it when she married Davey Montgomery. Georgina and Harry were no more than two or three at the time, so it made sense for them. I stayed a McPherson."

"Was that your choice?"

"Och, it wasn't a matter of choice. Davey didn't like me, and I didn't like him. He never offered me his name and I didn't want it."

Jack had been sitting stiffly beside her, but now Anne began to feel him unwind. He took several deep breaths and leaned towards Moira. "What was this Davey Montgomery like?" he asked.

"He didn't belt our mother, if that's what you're asking."

"I guess, in a roundabout way, that is what I'm asking."

"He didn't. He had a temper, mind, but I never saw him raise a hand to her. He never hit me or the wee bairns either. He left that to our mother."

"So he wasn't bad as a stepfather?" Jack asked.

"I never thought of him as a father of any kind, although the two young ones did," Moira said. "He treated them well enough, especially when he found out that my mother couldn't have more children. He decided they'd be his."

"What did he do for a living?" Jack asked.

"When I lived with them, he was a bookie. He worked for one of the Glasgow gangs, taking bets on the horses and the greyhounds before betting shops became legal. He was good with numbers. He taught Harry and Georgina adding and subtracting, and even multiplication and division. Both of them were smart, and they knew their maths before they even started school."

"Did they do well in school?"

"Well enough. They both ended up at Glasgow University."

"Do they still live in Scotland?" Anne asked.

"Why else would I ask if you were going off to see them?"

"Sorry, I should have remembered you said that," Anne said.

"In which part of the country do they live?" Jack asked.

"Harry is in Edinburgh. The last I heard, Georgina was in Bearsden, a fancy town just outside of Glasgow."

"She has a comfortable life?" he asked.

"She did have. I don't know about now."

"When was the last time you spoke to her?"

"Five or six years. I'm not really sure."

"And when did you last speak to Harry?"

"About two years ago."

"Are you closer to Harry?"

"I'm not close to either of them. Harry was in Irvine on some company business and dropped in to see me. As soon as he saw my situation, he scarpered off."

"How would I contact them if I wanted to?" Jack asked.

"I don't know."

"You don't have any phone numbers or addresses?"

"No."

"What company does Harry work for?"

"Caledonia Insurance. He's been there for years. He's some kind of manager."

"Does Georgina work?" Jack asked.

"Her husband has money."

"Do you know her husband's first name?"

"I do, but only because it's odd. He's an Atholl, like in Blair Atholl. It's a name you don't forget once you hear it."

"No, I don't imagine you would," Jack said. "Would you also happen to remember what Atholl does for a living?"

"He's a businessman of some sort."

"What kind of business?"

"Buying and selling, and don't ask me what because I don't know."

Jack leaned back against the sofa, closed his eyes, and pursed his lips. Anne knew he was in calculating mode.

"This has been very helpful. Thank you," Anne said quietly to Moira.

"I haven't done anything," she said.

Jack leaned forward again. "Moira, does Georgina or Harry know I exist?"

"I don't know."

"You never discussed me with them?"

"There was never a need."

"And how about our mother? Did she ever mention me to them?"

Moira looked at Jack in confusion. Then her face sagged in what Anne could only describe as pain. "I don't know how to answer that question," she said.

"Be honest," Jack said.

"I don't know what to say."

"Just tell me the truth, as best you can. I'm not going to get angry, no matter what you tell me."

Moira's eyes flitted between Jack and Anne as if asking one of them to tell her it was okay not to answer.

"Tell me, please," Jack said.

"Well, if I didn't make it clear earlier, let me do so now," she finally said, her voice trembling. "From about a week after she left the cinema until the day she died, I don't think your name ever passed our mother's lips again."

8

THEY DROVE IN SILENCE until they reached the outskirts of Troon. Anne finally said, as calmly as she could, "I am so sorry it turned out like that."

"Which part are you referring to?" Jack asked.

"All of it, but especially the part about your mother not mentioning your name."

"How could that be any more hurtful than what she did to me?"

"Still, it would have been nice if Moira had been more . . ."

"Untruthful?"

"I didn't mean that."

"Then what?"

"More sensitive. More like you. Not quite so downtrodden."

"She's a poorly educated working-class woman from the Gorbals. What should we have expected? The miracle is that I got out of this country. I might have ended up like her if I'd stayed."

"Do you think you'll ever see her again?"

He shook his head. "Why would I? She has nothing more to tell me and we have absolutely nothing in common. Truthfully, talking to her was painful."

"I hope you aren't overly disappointed."

"I had low expectations, but I won't deny that part of me was hoping there would be a connection worth sustaining," he said. "I will send her some money, though, when we get home."

"I hope I don't sound cruel, but if you don't want to stay connected with her, I'm a bit surprised that you would send her anything."

"I feel sorry for her. I had lumped her in with my mother, but when she started talking about the siblings and the second husband, I realized she'd been shunted aside like me. She's a rather pathetic woman."

"I would prefer it if you used the word *tragic*," Anne said. "She suffered in her own way from what your mother put you both through, but she wasn't as fortunate. She didn't have the Andersons; she had Davey Montgomery."

"Your ability to see multiple sides of a story never ceases to amaze me."

"I was raised to have an open mind. In some ways it's a curse, because people think you have no convictions."

"I'd never suggest that, not even when I'm desperate for you to take my side."

"And which side is that?"

"I want to understand the woman who was my mother and the man who was my father. I want to keep digging until there's nothing left to find," he said. "But I don't want to do it alone. However difficult it was with Moira, it would have been far worse if you hadn't been there. You helped build a bridge between us. I'm not much good at that kind of thing."

"Are you saying you want to go to Bearsden and Edinburgh, that you want to meet Georgina and Harry?"

Jack nodded, and she thought he looked slightly anxious. It pleased her that he still seemed to value her approval. "We need to locate them first," she said.

"It shouldn't be that hard. How many Atholl Malcolms could be living in Bearsden? And one phone call to the Caledonia Insurance Company in Edinburgh should unearth Harry Montgomery."

"But if we find them, how are you going to approach them? From what Moira said, they probably don't know you exist."

"Just like I didn't know they existed?"

"That's different. You were living on a different continent in a different world. They've been here, with the woman who was their mother and your mother. They might not believe it if she never told them about you."

"We only have Moira's story to go on, and it doesn't exactly sound like she was plugged into the family circle."

"Even if she didn't tell them and you're the one to break

the news, there are a million worse things someone could be told than that Bloody Jack Anderson is their older brother," she said.

His head swung towards her. "You know I dislike being called that."

"I'm sorry," she said quickly. "It slipped out."

"Does it slip out often?" he said, his voice agitated.

"Of course not, but every once in a while I hear it from one of the kids," she said. "And Jack, it's always said respectfully. Truly, I've never understood why it offends you so much."

"I dislike it because it implies that I used cutthroat tactics to grow Pilgrim."

"I never got that implication, and neither have the children. Mark says you're admired by his colleagues in Chicago."

"As much as I love my son, I've never been crazy about his chosen profession. Being admired by a bunch of unethical Chicago traders is not exactly an endorsement."

"That's not fair to Mark," she said sharply.

"No, I guess it isn't. I retract."

"Jack, I don't like it when you pretend to be a paragon of virtue. Don't tell me that you grew Pilgrim without occasionally cutting some corners, without making a few enemies."

"I have been disciplined, determined, and tightly focused," he said. "I don't see those as virtues, just good business practices."

Anne sighed and looked out the car window at a lush green landscape. "I hate it when we argue."

Jack started to say something, but he was approaching a roundabout that needed his full attention.

"We'll make some phone calls as soon as we get back to the hotel," Anne said, taking the opportunity to change the subject. "If we can reach either Harry or Georgina, there's no reason we can't go to Bearsden or Edinburgh today."

As they exited the roundabout, their hotel came into view. A few minutes later Jack parked the car and they walked to the hotel entrance, hand in hand.

"Are you hungry? Do you want some lunch?" he asked.

"No, I'm fine. I'd rather make those calls."

"Me too," Jack said.

They went directly to their suite. Jack sat at the desk while Anne sat across from him. He called the hotel operator and asked to be connected to information in Edinburgh. A moment later he had the number for Caledonia Insurance. He had never heard of the company, but that didn't mean it was insignificant. Jack's dealings were mainly in North America or with overseas industry goliaths. But instead of calling Caledonia, he phoned his assistant in Boston. It was seven a.m. there, but he knew Pam would be at her desk.

"This is Mr. Anderson's office," she answered.

"Pam, it's me. I need you to get me some information," he said. "There's an insurance company in Edinburgh called Caledonia. Find out what you can about it, and especially one of their executives, named Harry or Henry Montgomery. I'm in the Marine Hotel. Call me back as soon as you can. This has priority."

When she hung up, Jack contacted the hotel operator again. "I need the phone number for a Mr. Atholl Malcolm who lives in Bearsden," he said.

As he waited, he looked at the map of Scotland on the desk. Bearsden was north of Glasgow, about two-thirds of the way to Stirling. From Troon he calculated it would be a drive of about an hour and a half.

"I'm sorry, Mr. Anderson, we can't seem to find a listing for an Atholl Malcolm in Bearsden, or in any of the nearby towns and cities, including Glasgow," the operator said.

"Thank you for taking the time to look beyond Bearsden," he said. "Could I trouble you to see if there's a listing for a Georgina Malcolm in any of those locations?"

"Of course, Mr. Anderson. Hold, please."

He looked at Anne. "No listing for Atholl Malcolm in Bearsden or environs."

"Mr. Anderson, I haven't found a Georgina Malcolm, but there are several Georges and two G. Malcolms," the operator said.

"Where are the G. Malcolms?"

"Both are in Glasgow."

"I'd like those numbers, please."

He wrote them on a sheet of hotel stationery, thanked the operator, and hung up. A few seconds later the phone rang. "Hello," he said.

"Hi, this is Pam. I have the information you requested."

"Go ahead."

"Caledonia Life is a moderately sized, rather trad-itional insurance company. It was founded 110 years ago as a division of the Bank of Caledonia but split off as a completely separate business ten years ago. Its headquarters are on Lothian Road in Edinburgh. Harry Montgomery is vice-president of customer, shareholder, and government relations."

"So he's essentially a PR man?"

"Yes."

"Give me the company address and phone number, please."

"Yes, sir," she said, and then recited them. "Is there anything else I can do with regard to Caledonia?"

"No, I'll handle it from here. I'll talk to you tomorrow," he said, putting down the phone. "Well, we've found Harry Montgomery, and I'm quite sure he'll lead us to the sister."

"How are you going to approach him?" Anne asked.

"I don't know. It was easier with Moira because I had time and distance on my side. Until she wrote back to me she wasn't real, and even after I knew she was alive, I had several months to prepare myself mentally before meeting her," he said. "This is completely unexpected, so I'm not sure what to do. Do I phone? Do I drop in on him? How does one break this kind of news?"

"I think it should be done in person," she said. "And it would be silly of us to drive all the way to Edinburgh and discover that he's not in the office or off on holiday somewhere. So my suggestion would be to call his office and make an appointment to see him there, or maybe outside the premises."

"I would prefer not to meet at his office, but I'll need an excuse to meet with him in the first place," he said.

"Do you think it's possible he's heard of Pilgrim?"

"Yes, it is possible, and maybe even likely."

"Then is there some business reason you could contrive?"

"It couldn't be anything corporate. He's too junior for me to contact him directly about anything on that scale."

"Could you suggest that Pilgrim is thinking of expanding into the U.K. and talking to various local industry executives about their joining the company?"

"We'd do that far more discreetly, and we'd use a head-hunting outfit."

"Well, tell him you're on holiday and would like to take advantage of being in Edinburgh by sitting down with him for a coffee. Tell him you've already met several local insurance executives on a personal and confidential basis."

"I'm not sure . . ."

"Jack, you're making me work very hard here," she said. "If that won't do, you'll have to come up with an excuse on your own."

"It might work," he mused.

"Why don't I make the call for you," she said. "I'll say I'm your personal assistant."

"Yes. It would make sense that I approach him that way."

"Then give me the phone number." He passed the slip of paper to her.

She noticed his discomfort. "Maybe you should leave the room while I do this. You're making me nervous."

Please let Harry Montgomery be in his office, Anne thought as she dialled.

A woman answered. "Caledonia Insurance. How may I direct your call?"

"Mr. Harold Montgomery, please."

"Who should I say is calling?"

"Anne Aring," she said, using her maiden name. "I'm calling on behalf of Mr. Jack Anderson, CEO of Pilgrim Insurance in Boston, in the United States."

"One moment." Anne waited, listening to an instrumental rendition of the "Skye Boat Song."

A moment later she heard a soft burr. "This is Harold Montgomery. How can I help you, Miss Aring?"

"Mr. Montgomery, thank you for taking my call," she said. "I am personal assistant to Mr. Jack Anderson, the CEO of Pilgrim Insurance in Boston."

"I certainly know who Mr. Anderson is, but I'm quite at sea as to why you would be calling me on his behalf."

"Before I go any further, Mr. Montgomery, I have to ask if you're prepared to treat whatever I have to say in the greatest confidence," she said. "I assure you that it would in no way compromise your obligations to Caledonia, but I have to ask you anyway."

"I can do that," he said after a slight hesitation.

"Excellent. In that case, let me be straightforward," Anne said. "Mr. Anderson would like you to meet with him."

"Why?" Montgomery asked.

It was Anne's turn to pause. "I think it best if he explains that to you himself," she finally said. "All I'm allowed to say is that Pilgrim is exploring business opportunities in the U.K. and Mr. Anderson thinks you could be a valuable part of the process."

"Miss Aring, if Mr. Anderson is looking for information about Caledonia, I think a formal approach would be more appropriate. I would be reluctant to share that kind of information without the approval of my superiors."

Another one who's making it difficult for me, Anne thought. "Mr. Anderson has no interest in Caledonia. His interest is in you, as part of his U.K. team."

"But how—" Montgomery began.

"As I said, I think it's best for him to explain the details to you himself," she said. "Are you available later today?"

"No, I'm afraid not. I have an executive meeting that will go on all afternoon."

"How about this evening or tomorrow morning? And, obviously, it might be best if you met with him outside the office. Is there a café near your building that you could recommend?"

"This is most unconventional."

"I understand your reaction, but Mr. Anderson doesn't

place much value on convention," Anne said. "Now, what shall I tell him—this evening or tomorrow morning?"

"Tomorrow is better for me."

"And a place and time?"

"There's a Brava Coffee House on Drummond Street, northeast from our offices on Lothian. I could meet Mr. Anderson there at ten a.m."

"Consider it done. He'll see you there," she said, ending the conversation.

She sat at the desk for a moment, quietly pleased with herself, and was getting up to tell Jack what had transpired when he walked into the room.

"I didn't know you could act so well," he said.

"You heard?"

"I did. When do we meet him?"

"Tomorrow morning at ten in a coffee shop near his office."

"Thank you, that's terrific," he said, and then looked at his watch. "That means we have the rest of this afternoon and evening free."

"Do you have something in mind?"

"Glasgow is only thirty miles from here. I think I'd like to see my mother's grave in Govan," he said.

"Really?"

"Yes, if for no other reason than to confirm what Moira told us."

"Okay, let's do that," Anne said.

"There's one more thing," he said awkwardly.

"Yes?"

"I want to go to the Regal Cinema, the movie house where my mother left me."

She stared at him. "How do you know the name?"

"I can't explain it, but I do. I remember it quite clearly."

Anne walked towards him and took his hands in hers. "Jack, that was more than fifty years ago. What makes you think the place is still there?"

"I had Pam check."

"You didn't tell me."

"I did it a month ago. I was curious — nothing more than that at the time — but now that we're here and so close, I want to see it."

She wrapped her arms around his waist and pressed her head against his chest. "Then we'll visit the Regal Cinema."

9

IT WAS RAINING WHEN they left Troon, but the roads were well marked and Jack had no trouble following the directions they had been given by the hotel concierge. Both the Gorbals and Govan were in the southern part of Glasgow, and almost the same distance from Troon. Jack decided to go to Govan first. When they reached the city's outskirts, Anne spread a map on her lap and guided him through the streets to St. Andrew's Church and the cemetery.

"Everything looks so sturdy," Anne said as they passed row upon row of red, brown, and blond sandstone buildings topped with grey slate roofs.

"They're built to withstand the weather," Jack said.

"I wonder how many have central heating?"

"I'm sure most of them have it by now."

"I was surprised that Moira didn't, just as I was surprised by how few trees there are in Irvine — and here."

"You can't compare Glasgow to Wellesley Hills, with its half-acre lots and stands of trees," Jack said. "This is urban, more like Beacon Hill or Little Italy in Boston."

"I hope the graveyard has some greenery."

Fifteen minutes later Jack parked the car in front of St. Andrew's Church. The rain had stopped but the sky was dark and the air was heavy. He reached for his Red Sox cap as he looked out the window at a squat red-brick building with a modest bell tower. "For some reason I thought the church would be older," he said.

"And it looks so gloomy. I can't see a single tree or even a blade of grass."

The property was surrounded by a three-foot-high brick wall, its only visible entrance a wrought-iron gate. They got out of the car and went over to it. "The cemetery seems to be behind the church," Jack said, pointing to a sign beside a gravel walkway.

They opened the gate and walked along the side of the church towards the rear. Anne noticed that Jack was uneasy. "Are you sure you want to do this?" she asked.

"How much more harm can it do?"

"None."

"Besides, I want to stand on her grave."

Anne stopped. "Jack, that isn't like you."

He looked past her. "Sorry. I'm feeling a lot of mixed emotions right now."

"I'm also not used to you talking about your emotions."

"Would you prefer I didn't?"

"Of course not. I'm glad you're able to talk about how you're feeling," Anne said. "I just have to get used to it. And I will, so don't stop."

They reached the rear of the church. Between its back wall and a row of houses in the distance were lines of headstones set in a gravel bed. "This is far larger than I thought it would be," Anne said.

"At least it's orderly. It would be much more difficult to find her grave if people were buried haphazardly."

Anne did a quick count. There were twenty rows between them and the cemetery's outer boundary, and each row had about thirty graves. "Let's split up. I'll head to the back, you start at the front."

"Remember, the name on her headstone will be Jessie Montgomery, not McPherson," he said.

Anne nodded and walked to the rear of the cemetery. She was a history buff and had visited graveyards in many countries, although her favourite was close to home — the Granary Burying Ground in Boston, where Samuel Adams, John Hancock, and Paul Revere were buried. As she started along the last row of headstones at St. Andrew's, it soon became apparent there wasn't much history to be found. The oldest headstone was dated 1928, none of the names of the buried meant the slightest thing to her, and the headstones made no claims of significance. She soon stopped reading everything but the engraved names.

Jack was moving as quickly. They were separated by only two rows when he shouted, "Here it is."

Anne slipped between the headstones to reach Jack. He was staring down at a grey granite slab. It read:

HERE LIES JESSIE MONTGOMERY
MOTHER AND WIFE
BORN GLASGOW, MARCH 1909
DIED GLASGOW, JULY 1972

"She was just a bit older than sixty when she died, almost the same age I am now," Jack said.

"And if my math is correct, she was sixteen when she had Moira. She was still a girl — a child."

"So she was nineteen when she had me and twenty-five when she abandoned me. At twenty-five you're a woman, not a girl anymore. You're supposed to act like an adult."

Anne heard the bitterness in his voice and put aside a thought that had come to her as she read the headstone. Moira had said that her mother was a hard woman who'd had a hard life. The inscription on the stone was a testament to that. It was completely lacking in sentiment. Not a word about being loved or having loved, and not the slightest hint that she'd be missed. But rather than saying something that Jack might misconstrue as sympathy for his mother, all Anne said was, "She was certainly old enough to know better."

He shook his head. "I wish I hadn't come here."

"Then we should leave."

Jack turned abruptly from the grave and walked back

towards the car. Anne hurried to catch up. When she did, she slipped her arm through his. "Perhaps we shouldn't go to the movie house," she said.

"We're in Glasgow. We might as well finish what we started."

"I'm not sure that's such a good idea. I don't like to see you upset."

"It was just the shock of seeing her name. It made her real," he said.

"How will the movie house be any different?"

"Strange as it seems, I can remember it in my mind's eye — or at least I think I can. It was a big, dark, gloomy place that rather haunts me."

"So why visit?"

"Because it might not be as scary as I remember it, and then I can rid myself of that feeling. For sure it can't be any worse than this."

"I still don't like to see you upset."

"I guess I could pretend none of this affects me. If I was at home in Wellesley, surrounded by familiar things, that would be the natural thing for me to do," Jack said. "But there are things going on inside me that I can't control, and luckily I'm in a place where my loss of control doesn't matter a damn to anyone except you and me."

They drove away from St. Andrew's without a backward glance. Jack focused on the road ahead while Anne read the map and tried not to think about her husband's disquieting behaviour. She had rarely seen Jack lose his composure — Thanksgiving dinner had been one of the few times — but it seemed to her that he was now on the verge of doing so again.

Despite Pam's information, Anne wasn't completely convinced they'd find the Regal Cinema still intact, and as they drove past row after row of recently constructed apartment towers, her conviction grew. She knew from her reading that the Gorbals had been a famously dangerous slum until the 1960s, when the government razed large parts of it. The displaced residents were sent to towns like Irvine or put into new social housing in the Gorbals. Either way, the razing didn't seem to have done much for people's lives; the rates of poverty and violence in the Gorbals were still among the highest in the U.K.

The rain was intermittent and traffic was slow. As they neared the street that supposedly housed the Regal, they entered an area that was more commercial than any they'd passed through since leaving St. Andrew's. They passed a bakery, a butcher's shop, a tobacconist, newspaper stands, several coffee shops, a greengrocer, and an Italian restaurant with an ice cream shop. Some of the businesses looked as if they had been there for many years. Anne saw Jack eyeing them.

"We're getting close to the Regal. Is any of this familiar to you?" she asked.

"None of it."

"That's not surprising," she said, and added, "You need to turn left here."

As the car cleared the corner, the Regal Cinema — the Regal Revival Cinema, as it was now signed — came into view. Jack stopped the car by the curb directly across the street and stared at the theatre through a rain-spattered window. "It looks smaller than I remember," he said.

The movie house had a ticket window to the right of two glass double doors; a display case held posters advertising *Crocodile Dundee* and *A Room with a View*. The marquee above the doors simply read "Dundee."

"It reminds me of the cut-rate movie house I used to go to in Amherst when I was a student," Anne said. "It showed second-run films as well."

"Let's see if we can go inside," Jack said.

"It looks like it isn't open yet."

"We'll knock on the doors. Someone may answer."

Before Anne could respond, Jack stepped onto the sidewalk and started walking across the street. When she caught up to him, she found him already banging on the door. They waited, peering through the glass into a small, dingy lobby. When no one came, Jack knocked again.

"Maybe no one is here," Anne said a few minutes later.

"I'll give it one last go," Jack said, raising his hand.

As he did, a short, bald man wearing denim overalls over a black sweater walked into the lobby and looked at them. He approached the doors and said in a muffled voice, "We're closed."

"We don't want to see a film. I just want to see inside the theatre," Jack shouted.

"We're closed," the man repeated.

"I used to come here when I was a child. I have memories of this place. All I want to do is have a quick look inside," Jack said and reached for his wallet.

The man stared at the wallet.

Jack took out a twenty-pound note and held it against the glass. "Five minutes inside, that's all we need."

The man nodded, turned a lock, and one of the doors swung open. He reached for the money. "Five minutes, that's it. And don't touch anything."

Jack and Anne stepped into the carpeted lobby. In front of them was a concession stand with a glass case filled with candy and a pop dispenser. On either side of it were doors that Anne assumed led into the theatre. "What's that smell?" Jack asked.

Anne took a deep breath. "It's a musty smell, and the carpet feels a bit wet underfoot. I also smell mothballs."

"We've just had our annual cleaning. The carpets aren't dry yet," the man said.

"How old is this place?" Anne asked.

"It was built in 1932. There aren't many left like this. It's become a bit of a landmark."

"And you do enough business to stay open?"

"You'd be surprised how many people still like to go to the pictures, especially when it costs half of what they'd pay on the High Street."

"Let's go into the theatre," Jack said to Anne.

The man seemed surprised.

"I didn't give you twenty pounds just to stand here in the lobby," Jack said to him.

"Give me a minute to turn on the lights," he said. "You can go on in then, but make it quick."

The man left them standing in the lobby. Jack went over to the door on the left, opened it, and stared into darkness. Anne joined him, noticing that the smell of mothballs had become even stronger.

Lights began to flicker and come to life, exposing the drab interior. The theatre floor was sloped from back to front and covered with the same plain red carpet as the lobby. The walls were painted mustard yellow. There were about thirty rows of seats, twelve across. At one point in their lives the seats might have been covered in plush green velvet, but now the material was threadbare and the colour only a hint of what might have been. Jack began to walk down the aisle towards the front. Anne followed. From the back of the theatre the screen looked like a pristine sheet of white canvas, but as they got closer it began to resemble a quilt of sewn-together patches, albeit all of them some shade of white.

Jack stopped in front of the screen and looked back at the seats. "I was sitting somewhere in the middle of a row, somewhere in the middle of the theatre. At least, that's how I remember it," he said. "I had to kneel to see past the person in front of me. My mother sat between Moira and me. Going to the movies was a big deal. I had been maybe only twice before."

"You can really recall that?"

"I don't know if I'm recalling or imagining. I don't know what's real," he said as he began to walk back up the aisle, only to stop halfway. "I can see my mother leaning over me and whispering that she had to take Moira to the bathroom. Then her kissing me on the forehead and telling me that she loved me."

Anne reached for his hand. It was sweaty.

"What kind of mother kisses a child, tells him he's loved, and then dumps him like a bag of garbage?" he said.

"Jack, I don't know what to say."

He removed his hand from hers and sat down in an aisle seat. "One good thing is that this place seems much less threatening than I've been imagining it."

"How long has it been on your mind?"

"For months. The instant I started thinking about Moira, all this came back to me."

"But you said you don't know if things happened the way you think they did."

"Even if I'm not sure about the details, the feelings they generate are real."

"Of course they are," Anne said. "And shame on her for what she did to cause them."

10

IT WAS DARK WHEN they arrived back at the Marine Hotel. They hadn't talked much during the drive from Glasgow as Anne focused on the map and Jack concentrated on driving on the opposite side of unfamiliar roads. But she thought he seemed the most relaxed he had been all day. She wondered if visiting the graveyard and the movie house had exorcised some demons.

"Do you want to have dinner in the hotel or shall we go into town?" Anne asked as they pulled into the hotel parking lot.

"Let's eat here. I have a real thirst for some Scotch and I don't want to worry about driving."

"I need to freshen up a bit, and I told Allison I'd call to tell her about our day."

"Do you have to call?"

"No."

"Then do me a favour and hold off until we meet this

Harry Montgomery. You could have something more concrete to tell her then."

"She's going to be shocked. They all will be. Suddenly their father has three siblings, not one, and they might have a horde of cousins they never knew existed."

"That's why I want you to wait. Let's find out what's what."

"I guess that's wisest."

Twenty minutes later they were sitting in the hotel dining room sipping their first drinks. Jack had ordered a double Johnnie Walker Black on the rocks; Anne had a gin martini with olives. They finished them in quick order, ordered a second round, and then looked at the menu while the waiter hovered nearby.

"Haddock in cream sauce with boiled potatoes for me," Anne said.

"Steak and kidney pie," Jack said.

"Wine this evening?" the waiter asked.

"I think you should just keep refilling our drinks until we tell you otherwise," Jack said.

"You're going to get me drunk," Anne said when the waiter had left.

"Like the old days, before the kids started to arrive."

"I think we were both drunk when we conceived Allison."

"Luckily there's no chance of conceiving anyone tonight."

"Are you saying you won't ravish me when we get back to our room?"

"I'm not promising anything of the sort," Jack said with an awkward smile.

Anne smiled in return, knowing full well there was little chance of that happening. Their sex life had mostly disappeared, without any real acknowledgement that it was gone. "How do you feel about the day?" she asked.

"It wasn't what I expected."

"Is that good or bad?"

"It's too soon to tell."

"Can I tell you what I was just thinking?" she asked.

He knew it was pointless to say no because she'd tell him anyway. "Of course."

"I was thinking about Martin and Colleen and how marvellous they were."

"Because they took in an orphan at an age when many orphans are shunned?"

"No, because they took in a young boy and then loved him and nurtured him the way they did. They must have been ambitious for you, but I can't remember you ever telling me you felt pressured to succeed."

"On the surface they were just ordinary people. He was a plumber, like his father, and she was a cashier at a grocery store. But they both read constantly. The *Boston Globe* from cover to cover every day, magazines of all sorts, books — oh my god, the books they read. They didn't read every one in the Watertown Library, but they sure as hell tried, and they weren't bashful about recommending books to me."

"Who read more?"

"Mom, but she preferred fiction and I didn't always agree with her taste," he said. "Dad was keener on non-fiction, especially history and biographies. He thought there were lessons to be drawn from the past and from the lives of successful people. He wanted me to understand that when it comes to the way people behave, there isn't much new in this world, and to realize that what people achieve is directly related to the amount of thought and effort they put into it. I know that sounds trite, but I bought into it then and I still buy into it now."

"And they put their money where their mouths were."

"They did. I was the first member of either of their families to go to university, and they paid for my entire six years at Bentley and for a car to get me there and back."

"I remember when I met you how astounded I was that you had no college debt. Nearly everyone else I knew was up to their armpits in it."

"They wanted me to start my career with a clean slate. They wanted me to look forward, not backward. They wanted me to take a job that interested me and had a future, not to be worrying about the size of my first paycheque."

Anne sipped her martini. Then, without looking directly at her husband, she asked, "Would your success have been possible if you'd stayed here?"

"How can I answer a question like that?"

"I mean in theory, given the class structure here, who your parents were, seeing how Moira turned out."

"What brought this on?"

"Meeting Moira."

"An unfortunate woman."

"A product of her environment."

"A great many people have been able to overcome their environment."

"That's easy to say when you've done it. Not so easy when you're trapped in it and don't even understand there are ways out."

Jack looked annoyed but silently sat back in his chair as the waiter arrived with fresh drinks. "Cheers," he said, raising his new glass.

Anne tapped her glass against his. "I'm sorry for going on like that. I think I have jet lag."

"And I'm sorry if I seem out of sorts," he said. "I know your mother never worked outside the home, and I know she thought—despite wanting you to have a fine education—that a woman's true role is in the home as a wife and mother."

"I'm perfectly content with the life I've led, and I'm looking forward to our next chapter together when you retire," she said, and then hesitated. "Although I'd be dishonest if I said I don't have concerns about how we're going to get along when we're under the same roof for extended periods of time."

"Why would you worry about that?"

"Jack, for close to forty years you've spent five days a week at the office and part of every weekend working at home or travelling on Pilgrim business. I'm not complaining; I'm just stating it as a fact," she said. "During those years I developed my own routines, first when the children were at home and then later, after they left. There's a rhythm to my days that I'm comfortable with."

"Are you afraid I'll disrupt it?"

"A little bit."

"Don't be. I'll have lots to do."

"Like what?"

"What do you mean?"

"I mean, what are you going to do?" she asked. "Mark and I talked about it at Thanksgiving. You have no hobbies, and we don't see you suddenly taking up golf or sailing. Your entire life has been consumed by Pilgrim. How do you intend to transition from being totally absorbed in your career to doing . . . nothing?"

"It won't be nothing. I've been approached to sit on some boards. I have an interest in several charities. I have a long list of books I'll now have time to read."

"Given your energy level and intellectual capacity, Mark doesn't think that will be enough. I have to say I'm inclined to agree with him."

"What would you have me do? Not retire?"

"No, but it does seem to me that you haven't given it a lot of thought."

"I've had a lot of other things on my mind. That's one

reason we're here," he said. "Once this is behind us, I'll start focusing more on matters such as what I'm going to do when I'm retired."

The arrival of their meals brought the conversation to a temporary halt. The waiter eyed their drinks as he put plates in front of them.

"When these drinks are gone, bring us one more round," Jack said to him.

"You may have to carry me upstairs," Anne said.

"It's the least I can do."

Anne smiled. "I'm sorry if I'm being a nag, but I do worry about you."

"I know, and I'm grateful, even if it doesn't seem that way sometimes."

"One more nag?"

It was his turn to smile. "Sure."

"According to my map it's about a two-hour drive to Edinburgh, so we should leave the hotel by seven-thirty tomorrow at the latest. That means an early start to the day," she said. "I won't function very well if I drink much more, and I don't think you will either. So let's make this our last and head directly upstairs when dinner is finished."

"Yes, boss."

11

JACK WOKE UP EARLY again. He retrieved an envelope
that had been slipped under the door and sat at the desk to
go over its contents. When he had finished, he called Pam's
office line to leave his comments. He had promised Anne
he wouldn't work on this trip, but then later modified it
to say he wouldn't work on Pilgrim business when he was
with her. That left him only the hours she was sleeping,
which provided a very small window of opportunity. Part
of him chafed at being so restricted, but the realist in him
knew that, if left to his own devices, he would work most
of the day. He didn't think of himself as a workaholic. He
was simply a man who loved what he was doing, and what
he was doing at the moment was running a company that
was having a record year for sales, profits, and growth.

When he had left his last instructions for Pam, he went
to the window. It was still dark outside — and would be
until Anne's alarm went off at seven — but the lights in the

parking lot illuminated the outer edges of the golf course. Golf wasn't Jack's game. It took too much time to play, and much more time to practise if you wanted to be halfway competent at it. Being competent had never been one of Jack's goals in anything. If he couldn't be first-rate, he had no interest in the pursuit. He didn't know how to explain that to Anne, who was one of the least competitive people he knew. Still, he admired her intelligence and intuition; her comments the night before about his not giving enough thought to retirement were bang on. What he hadn't said in response was that his reluctance to do so was because he was regretting the decision to retire and had started thinking about ways to postpone it.

Jack had been president and CEO of Pilgrim for twenty years, after persuading the board of directors to get rid of the previous CEO, Bob Young. But at the time Young was no longer capable of running the company, while at present Jack felt he had never been more capable. He had transformed Pilgrim from a mid-sized regional company to one with a strong national presence. It was now one of the top five insurance firms in the United States and was on track to become one of the Big Three. Jack wanted to see that achieved, and no one was better equipped to make it happen than him. The problem was that he had already told the board he was going to retire, and the decision had been announced publicly. As much as he regretted it now, at the time it had seemed the proper thing to do.

Jack's executive vice-president, Norman Gordon, had been named as his replacement. Gordon was capable but lacked vision. He also preferred to lead by consensus rather than by conviction and tended to avoid confrontation. Jack thought Gordon wouldn't put up much opposition if he decided to delay his departure and postpone Gordon's assumption of power.

The board might be a different story. When he announced his retirement, there had been some minor resistance from a few members, but mainly they went along with it. What would they do if Jack reversed his decision? He imagined that a few members were capable of digging in their heels and invoking the twenty-year limit. The only sure way for him to stay on with his image and legacy intact was for the board to ask him to serve for another year, or better yet, a few more years.

Jack had allies on the board but he'd never been a glad-hander or a backslapper, and he'd never felt the need to become close friends with its members. His attitude had always been to let the company's bottom line speak for him. Who could he call? Which of them might be open to the idea of his staying on? Which of them might be prepared to make the case for his remaining to their fellow board members?

"What are you thinking about?"

He stepped back from the window, startled and unsure for a second where he was. Anne stood in the bedroom doorway. "The day ahead," he said.

She nodded. "It's just past seven. Have you ordered coffee yet?"

"I'll do it now."

Half an hour later, Jack drove the car out of the hotel parking lot and pointed it in the direction of Edinburgh. They hadn't had much further chance to talk as they took turns in the bathroom and bedroom while the other ate toast and drank coffee.

As they cleared the last of the roundabouts and turned onto the highway that would take them to Edinburgh, Anne finally spoke. "Have you thought about how you're going to introduce yourself to your brother?"

"I can hardly think of him as that yet. He's a stranger."

"A stranger who you're going to inform is your brother."

"That's my intention, but I thought I'd try to ease into it."

"Easing into it may make for some initial awkwardness."

"I don't mind that. I'd prefer initial awkwardness to me just blurting it out."

"Either way, it will come as a shock to him."

"If we believe what Moira told us."

"You don't?"

"I wonder if we're putting too much stock in her memory," Jack said. "What if Harry and Georgina do know I exist? Maybe my mother did tell them about me."

"Moira is all we have to go on until you sit down with Harry."

"And one more thing. I've been thinking about her story about our mother being pregnant when she left me," he said.

"You don't think it's true?"

"It's possible, but who's to know who the father was? She said it was McPherson, but what if someone else fathered Harry and Georgina and that's the real reason she left?"

"You called him McPherson."

"What?"

"You just referred to your father as McPherson."

"What else do you suggest? I'm not calling him Dad."

"Fair enough," Anne said. "Maybe Harry can shed some light on this. And speaking of him, I wonder if there will be any physical resemblance between the two of you. You and Moira obviously don't look like siblings, but maybe it will be different with him. It's logical that there might be some similarities. We should have asked Moira if she had any photos of him or Georgina."

"It's a bit late for that now."

"She might even have had some photos of your mother," Anne said.

Jack's brow furrowed. "If she does, they're of no interest to me. And Harry and Georgina will get the same answer."

"Can I ask why?"

"You just have," Jack said.

"And?"

"I don't want to talk about it," he said with a firmness Anne knew was his way of telling her to stop pursuing the subject.

She turned away from him and looked out at the countryside. They had driven past several small towns, and the highway was now flanked by lush green fields. "It's so pretty here," she said.

"Pretty, but poor," Jack said. "Their biggest export for decades has been people."

Anne didn't reply and continued to look out the window. Jack's bad mood was beginning to get on her nerves. He had obviously decided to remain negative about Moira and dismissive of his mother. She wasn't about to argue with him just before meeting his brother, but neither did she want to talk about the failings of the Scottish economy.

They didn't speak again until an hour later, when they reached the outskirts of Edinburgh and Jack needed her to direct him to Drummond Street. A good navigator, she got them to a parking spot near the coffee shop shortly before ten. "Do you want to wait in the car or go right in?" she asked.

"There's no point in waiting. Besides, I could use a coffee."

"Are you sure you want me to come in with you? Might it be better for you to meet Harry on your own?"

"I want you there."

"Then let's go," Anne said, opening her door.

They approached the Brava Coffee House rather tentatively, stopping to look through its large plate-glass window. Inside they saw six square tables set against the wall, another ten smaller round tables spread across the floor, and a service counter close to the door. Most of the tables were occupied. Anne scanned them, looking for a man sitting by himself. There were several, but none of them resembled Jack or matched her idea of how an executive with an insurance company would dress.

Jack opened the door and went inside. "I'm meeting a man named Harold Montgomery," he said to the woman behind the counter. "Do you know if there's anyone here by that name?"

"I know Harry. He isn't here yet."

"Then we'll wait," Jack said, and turned to Anne. "Coffee?"

"A double espresso," she said.

"And I'll have a black coffee."

"Sugar or milk?" the server asked.

"Just plain."

"Find a table. I'll bring the coffees to you when they're ready," the woman said.

Two of the square tables were available, one near the window and the other in the rear of the shop. Jack led Anne towards the one at the back, which had four chairs. He sat so he had a clear view of the door. Anne sat next to him and then positioned her chair so it faced the same direction.

"It's convenient that the woman knows him," Jack said. "I was worrying about how we'd recognize him."

Anne smiled. "Jack, I'm quite sure he will have researched you and has some idea how you look. And even if he didn't, the Red Sox cap is a dead giveaway."

A few minutes later the woman brought two cups to the table. She put them down, began to leave, and then came to a stop after a couple of steps. "There's Harry now," she said, turning towards Jack and Anne. "He's the dapper one at the door, in the grey suit."

Anne blinked in surprise and glanced at Jack, expecting a similar reaction. His face was impassive. *Doesn't he see the similarities?* she thought. Harry was slightly shorter and slimmer than Jack, but he had the same square jaw, the broad brow supported by thick black eyebrows, and the same wide-set eyes.

She expected Jack to get up to greet Harry. When he didn't move, she rose from her chair and walked towards him. "Hi, I'm Anne. We spoke on the phone yesterday."

"Hello. Very pleased to meet you," Harry said, and then looked past her towards Jack. She saw him frown. Was he seeing the family resemblance?

The server squeezed past them. "Same as usual, Harry?" she asked.

"That's fine, love," he said.

"Come and join us, please," Anne said.

Jack stood and extended his hand. "Mr. Montgomery."

"Harry, please."

"And I'm Jack Anderson."

"I know who you are. It's an honour to meet you."

"Hardly an honour," Jack said. "Have a seat."

The two men sat across from each other, with Anne stuck uncomfortably between them.

"You'll have to excuse me if I appear nervous," Harry said. "Your call yesterday came out of the blue, and as I said to your assistant, this is quite unconventional."

"Anne isn't my assistant," Jack said, and then waited as the server placed a cup in front of Harry.

"She's with a headhunting firm?" Harry asked.

"No, she's my wife."

"This becomes even more unconventional," Harry said, glancing at Anne.

"Tell me, Harry, how long have you been with Caledonia?" Jack said quickly.

"My entire career. I joined the firm directly out of university."

"Are you an accountant?"

"I am, but that was my second degree. My first was in communications."

"That's an unusual combination."

"I wanted to go into public relations, but when I gradu-ated there weren't any jobs in that field, so I went back to school and took accounting. Who was to know I'd end up being able to combine the two disciplines?"

Jack nodded and sipped his coffee. Anne could see his discomfort and guessed he was buying time as he figured out what to say next. Small talk had never been his strong suit. Harry didn't look any more comfortable as he glanced rather absently around the coffee shop.

"Are you married?" Anne asked.

Both men looked surprised. Anne didn't know if that

was because of the nature of her question or the fact she'd spoken at all.

"Aye, I am, and quite happily, for more than twenty-five years," Harry said finally. "We have two children, Alastair and Ellen. They're both away at university."

"Are they following in their father's or mother's footsteps?" she said.

"Neither. Alastair wants to be an architect and Ellen is pursuing a career in medicine," he said. "My wife, Barbara, is a schoolteacher. She had hopes that Ellen would follow that career path, but since she was ten, all our daughter wanted was to be a doctor."

"How wonderful that your children know what they want and have been able to pursue it," Anne said. "Was education encouraged in your family?"

Harry glanced questioningly at Jack. When all he got in return was a curious stare, he said, "Very much so."

"Do you come from a large family?"

He shook his head. "I have one sister."

"Does she have children?"

"One daughter," Harry said, sounding slightly confused. "Although I don't understand—"

"Harry, you'll have to excuse my wife for asking such personal questions," Jack interrupted, leaning closer. "But the thing is, I wanted to meet you for an entirely different reason than the one Anne gave you on the phone yesterday."

"This isn't about a job?"

"It isn't, and I apologize for the subterfuge."

"Then what is it about?"

"Anne and I came to Scotland to piece together my family tree," Jack said.

"What does that have to do with me?" Harry said.

"I think you and your sister are part of that tree."

"Are you serious?"

"I couldn't be more serious. I think we're related."

"Well, that's a bit of a shock," Harry said, and then frowned in a way that reminded Anne of Jack. "But as nice as that might be, I'm not aware of any Andersons in our background."

"Anderson is my adopted name," Jack said. "My birth name was McPherson. Moira McPherson — who I don't think you included when you said you have one sister — is my sister as well. I believe we are brothers."

Harry reached blindly for his cup, almost tipping it over.

"I'm sorry to spring this on you, but your existence was a shock to me as well," Jack said. "After many years of not acknowledging my past, last year I finally began to come to terms with it and managed to track down Moira. Anne and I came to Scotland to visit her and she told us about you and Georgina. I didn't know about you until then, and that was only yesterday."

"You're Jack McPherson," Harry blurted.

"You know about me?"

"Of course I do," he said, staring across the table.

"Moira seemed to think you didn't."

"Moira and my mother were estranged for nearly all of Moira's adult life. She has no idea what went on in our house," he said. "When I said I have one sister, I was quite deliberately excluding Moira. We've had our issues. I don't think of her as part of the family anymore."

"Your relationship with Moira doesn't interest me, but your—our mother does. Are you saying she spoke about me?"

"She did, especially later in her life, and most often to Georgie. She desperately wanted to know what had become of you."

"Did she make any effort to find out?"

"Not directly. She was housebound, and she wouldn't have had any notion where to start," Harry said. "But I'll tell you what she did do—she ignited Georgie's interest. My sister has been looking for you for years."

"Well, here I am."

Harry shook his head again. "I'm having trouble believing this."

"Moira told us that our mother was pregnant with you and Georgina when she left McPherson. Is that the story you were told?"

"Yes."

"When were you born?"

"March fifth, 1935."

"That fits. So it seems that in addition to Moira, I've acquired a brother and another sister as well."

"Georgie is going to be thrilled."

"Has she really been looking for me?" Jack asked.

"She has, but I don't know about the details. You can ask her yourself when you meet her."

"Where does she live?" Anne asked.

"Here in Edinburgh, in the Stockbridge area. I live in Leith. We're only a ten-minute drive."

"Moira thought she was in Bearsden."

"She was until her husband left the country and she was forced to sell the house."

"Why did he leave?" Jack asked.

"I'll leave it to Georgie to tell you that story."

"When can we meet her?"

"I'll call her as soon as I get back to my office," Harry said. "Where are you staying?"

"In Troon."

"For any particular reason?"

"Only that it's close to Prestwick Airport and Irvine."

"It's not very convenient if you intend to spend time in Edinburgh."

"What do you suggest?"

"Take a hotel in Edinburgh. We have good corporate rates at several of them. You could return to Troon for your luggage and be back here by mid-afternoon."

Jack looked at Anne. "What do you think?"

"It makes sense to stay here."

"Shall I book you a hotel?" Harry asked.

"No, thank you, I prefer to do it myself," Jack said. "How will we stay in touch?"

"Call me at the office when you get to Troon. By then I'll have spoken to Georgie. Knowing her, she'll want to see you right away. Are you free this evening?"

"Yes, we're available."

"Fantastic. Maybe we can organize a wee family dinner tonight."

"That sounds like a plan."

Harry looked across the table at Jack and then turned to Anne. "When I spoke to you yesterday, I never would have imagined this. It's like something out of a film."

"Except it's real."

"Or surreal."

"Only because it's so sudden. Jack corresponded with Moira, so they had a few months to adjust to the idea before they met. This was just dropped on you. I think you've handled it very well, given the circumstances."

"It's hardly bad news."

"That is true," Anne said, smiling.

Jack looked at his watch. Anne knew it was a signal that he wanted to leave. "If we want to get back here this afternoon, I think we should start making tracks," he said to her.

She stood up and the men followed suit. No one moved at first, all of them unsure of what to do next. Then Jack thrust his hand towards Harry. "I'm pleased about the way this went," he said.

Harry nodded as he took Jack's hand. They shook for ten seconds, neither of them wanting to be the first to let go.

Anne turned to Harry and held out her arms. He withdrew his hand from Jack's and stepped towards her. She wrapped her arms around him. "We are a family that's big on hugs," she said.

12

IT TOOK THEM A while to disengage at the coffee shop, and there were a few minutes of awkwardness on the sidewalk before they went their separate ways. Finally Jack and Anne were alone in the car, heading back to Troon.

"That was something special," she said. "I don't think it could have gone any better."

"It went well enough," Jack said, and then looked at her. "Thank you for making it easier for me to tell him. The questions you asked about his family provided the perfect segue."

"Thank you, sweetheart," she said with a smile. "But I'm happy we won't have to do this again."

"Yes. Thank God Harry is going to tell Georgina. It was more stressful than I expected," he said. "Tell me, what did you think of Harry?"

"Do you mean aside from the fact that you have the same chin, forehead, and eyebrows?"

"Was the physical resemblance really that obvious?"

"Anyone could see it," she said. "What did you think of him?"

"I was pleased that Moira's story matched his account, and his birthdate is consistent with the timeline," he said. "As for what kind of person he is, it's too soon to tell. He seems decent enough. At least he has an education, a career, and a stable family life. I'm not so sure about his sister. I was a bit perturbed by what Harry said about her husband's behaviour. Why would he leave his wife in such a bad situation?"

"I'm sure she'll get around to telling you."

"I just hope it isn't anything unsavoury."

"Don't think the worst."

"It's hard not to. People don't leave their family and country without a reason."

"True, but don't start imagining a problem before you have some facts."

"Anticipating problems is part of what made me such a good CEO."

"Except here you aren't the CEO of anything. You're a man trying to connect with his family. As you discovered with Moira, you aren't going to find perfection."

Jack stared at the road. Anne saw his jaw stiffen and knew she had annoyed him. "I found it heartening that your mother wondered what had happened to you, and that Georgie has been looking for you," she said.

"I agree with you about Georgie."

"Good, because I sense that Georgina and her mother

were close. Maybe she'll be able to answer some of your questions about her."

The sky had been grey with a few blue streaks when they left Edinburgh, but now the blue disappeared entirely and rain teemed down. The windshield wipers could barely keep up with the downpour. The visibility was so bad that Jack considered pulling over, but he couldn't see where to do that safely, and so kept going. "I should concentrate on driving," he said. "We can talk later."

It took half an hour longer than their trip to Edinburgh to get back to Troon. The rain was beginning to let up when they reached the hotel, so they didn't get too wet walking from the parking lot. Jack went immediately to the concierge. "I'm afraid we have to cut short our stay here. Something has come up in Edinburgh that needs our attention. Can you recommend a hotel there?"

"Do you have any preferences as to cost and amenities?" the concierge said.

"I want the best hotel you can find. I don't care about the cost."

"That would be the North British on Princes Street, in the heart of the city. It's close to the castle and other sights," he said. "Do you want me to check for a vacancy?"

"Yes, do that. If there's a suite available, go ahead and book it," Jack said. "We're going upstairs to pack."

When they reached their room, Jack went directly to the desk, found the number for Caledonia, and dialled it. A moment later Harry came on the line.

"Have you spoken to Georgie?" Jack asked.

"Several times. She's so excited she keeps calling me back."

"Are we going to see her tonight?"

"Of course. My wife and I would like you and Anne to come to our house for dinner. Georgie and her daughter, Elizabeth, will join us."

"That's very kind of you, but we could go out to eat if that's more convenient."

"No, we insist that you come here. It will be less formal."

"All right, we will come for dinner," Jack said. "It'll be nice to meet Georgie and Elizabeth in a more casual environment. By the way, how old is Elizabeth? We didn't discuss Georgie's family earlier, except for her husband."

"Liz is Georgie's only child. She's in her early twenties. An aspiring actress."

"Anne dabbled in that when she was young, and we have a son-in-law who works in the film industry in Los Angeles."

"I wouldn't tell Georgie about your son-in-law. She can be a bit pushy when it comes to helping Liz."

"You know best," Jack said. "We should be back in Edinburgh by late afternoon. What time do you want to see us for dinner?"

"Seven would be dandy. Where are you going to stay?"

"The concierge is making a booking for us at the North British."

"That's a wonderful old railway hotel, but the route from there to my house is a bit complicated," Harry said.

"I think it would be best if I picked you up in my car, say around quarter to seven."

"That's fine with me."

"Then we're set. If you change your plans, you can reach me here at the office until five. After that you can call me at home. Here's the number," Harry said, and rattled it off.

Jack put down the phone and saw Anne looking at him from the bedroom door. "What did I dabble in?" she asked.

"Acting. Georgie has a daughter who wants to be an actress. We're meeting both of them tonight over dinner at Harry's house. He's picking us up at our hotel."

"Being a member of the dramatic society at UMass hardly qualifies as acting."

"It gives you a little something in common."

"If you say so. Now we need to finish packing. Do you want me to take care of your case?"

"Please. I'm going to call the concierge."

Twenty minutes later they left the hotel with their suitcases and a reservation for a suite at the North British Hotel. "I'm looking forward to Edinburgh. I just hope we're done with surprises," Anne said as the car left Troon.

13

IT WAS ALREADY DARK at six-forty as Jack and Anne stood outside the North British Hotel waiting for Harry. Behind them loomed the brightly lit Victorian stone and brick edifice. Over their heads the Union Jack and St. Andrew's Cross above the hotel entrance fluttered in the wind.

In Jack's opinion the hotel wasn't quite as wonderful as the concierge had promised. Its two-hundred-foot clock tower was spectacular and its location less than a mile from Edinburgh Castle ideal, but the building was more than eighty years old. Its age was showing in faded curtains, thinning carpets, and well-used furniture. In its prime it might have been one of the U.K.'s greatest railway hotels, Jack thought, but the only feature that impressed him was the massive tower with its clock hands permanently set three minutes fast to aid travellers.

"I should have asked Harry what kind of car he drives,"

Jack said as they watched a steady parade of cars and taxis pass.

Anne's arm was looped through Jack's. She looked up at him but didn't respond to his comment. He was on edge, like he'd been that morning during their drive to Edinburgh. She wasn't accustomed to seeing him like this; it suggested that discovering this larger family had made more of an impact on him than he was willing to admit.

"I think he's here," Jack said, interrupting her thoughts.

A green Jaguar came to a stop directly in front of the hotel and Harry waved at them from the driver's seat. Jack opened the back door for Anne and then climbed into the front passenger seat. "Right on time," he said.

"Traffic was light, and I did leave a bit early," Harry said. "Everyone is eager to meet you."

"Will your children be there?" Anne asked.

"No. Both of them attend universities in England, but you can be sure I'll be telling them about the new American branch of our family," Harry said. "By the way, we didn't talk about it this morning—how large is your family?"

"We have three children and two grandchildren," Anne said. "I'm an only child, so until a few months ago my children were under the impression that they had no aunts, uncles, or cousins. Then Jack told us about Moira, so they acquired an aunt. Now we're adding six more relatives."

"Have you told them yet?"

"We thought we'd wait until we'd met you and Georgie," Jack said.

Harry nodded and then tooted his horn at a slow-moving truck as he made a left turn. They had left the city centre quickly and were now passing rows of low-rise housing with street-level shops. Jack saw a sign indicating that Leith was two miles further.

Harry drove straight for about a minute and then started making right- and left-hand turns in an almost dizzying fashion until they found themselves in a small cul-de-sac. Harry's house was built of brick, with a red slate roof, a large window to the left of the front door, and three windows across the front of the second storey. The door was etched frosted glass and the downstairs window had drawn lace curtains.

Jack didn't see a second car. "How did Georgie get here?" he asked.

"By taxi," Harry said.

"She doesn't have a car?"

"She had to give it up."

"Because of the husband?" Jack asked.

"It doesn't matter why she had to give it up," Anne said. "Besides, not everyone needs a car. I've read that public transport is very good in the U.K."

"It is quite efficient," Harry said as he turned off the car, and climbed out.

Anne tapped Jack on the shoulder before he could get out. He turned to face her. "Stop asking questions about the husband," she whispered. "This isn't the time."

"Okay, but if the opportunity presents itself—"

"Do what my mother used to tell my father to do. Think twice about what you're going to say, and then don't say it."

"I hear you," he said with a noncommittal shrug.

They joined Harry on the gravel path that led to the front door. Anne could see the blurred outlines of two people behind the frosted glass. As they approached the door, it opened. A short, stout woman wearing a knee-length tartan skirt and a dark blue cardigan smiled at them. "Hello, I'm Barbara Montgomery," she said.

"Hi, I'm Anne Anderson," she replied, looking past Barbara at the much taller and thinner woman standing behind her. Anne took in the square chin, wide brow, and thick, tousled hair. "You don't have to tell me who you are."

"Likewise," Georgie said to Anne, but her eyes were focused on Jack.

"Come in, come in," Barbara said, stepping to one side.

They crowded into a narrow hallway that led to the kitchen. To the right was a stairway and on the left a door that opened into the living room. Anne thought the second door further down probably opened onto the dining room. She had been raised in a house exactly like it.

Barbara stood by the living room door, motioning for the others to join her. Harry and Anne did, but Jack and Georgie hesitated. "Harry was right. You do have some of our physical traits," Georgie finally said.

"Since I'm older, it's probably more proper to say you have some of mine," Jack replied.

Georgie burst into a loud, throaty laugh. Anne examined her more closely. Her features were broad and bony, and a mass of hair hung around her face and fell loosely to her shoulders. She was quite tall, at least five foot ten, and had a generous build beneath her white silk blouse. She was what the ladies of the Junior League in Wellesley might refer to as a handsome woman.

"Please, come into the living room," Barbara said.

They filed into a room with a fireplace in the far wall. Two large sofas upholstered in a purple and green plaid flanked the fireplace, separated by a large mahogany coffee table. A mahogany buffet laden with liquor and wine stood behind one of the sofas. Two chairs sat next to it.

Jack and Anne sat on the sofa with their backs to the window. Georgie sat across from them. Harry took one of the chairs, placing it at the end of the coffee table furthest from the fireplace.

"I'll be right back. I have some wee nibbles prepared in the kitchen," Barbara said.

"Is your daughter going to be joining us?" Anne asked Georgie.

"She wanted to, but something came up at the last minute," Georgie said. "If you're staying in Edinburgh for a few more days I'm sure you'll get a chance to meet."

"Drinks for everyone?" Harry interrupted.

"White wine for me," Georgie said.

"And me," said Anne.

"I'll have a Scotch," Jack said.

"How do you take it? American style?"

"Which is what, exactly?"

"On ice or with mix. Here we tend to drink it neat, or perhaps with a splash of water."

"On ice will be perfect."

As Harry went over to the buffet, Barbara returned carrying a large tray. "A selection of some of our Scottish cheeses and crackers," she said, and then sat next to Georgie. "I can't ever remember so much excitement in the house."

"It's been an emotional day for me as well," Jack said.

"I've been looking for you, you know," Georgie said. "I've been looking for you for years."

"That's what Harry said."

"I never imagined you'd turn up like this, completely out of the blue," she said. "And on top of that, you're famous."

"I'm hardly famous."

"Harry says you are."

"Harry is being too kind."

"Actually, I'm not," Harry said as placed three glasses of wine on the table. "Even on this side of Atlantic, people in our business know about Bloody Jack Anderson."

"Jack doesn't like being called that," Anne said.

"I don't know why. I love it," Georgie said. "How many people have a nickname, especially one that's so dashing?"

"I'd prefer not to talk about it," Jack said.

"Yes, let's drop it. I really shouldn't have mentioned it in the first place," Harry said as he returned with two glasses of Scotch. He handed one to Jack and then slowly raised his. "Here's to family. Old family and new family and what should have been family long before now."

"*Slàinte mhath*," said Georgie.

They all drank. Then Anne asked, "Georgie, when did you start looking for Jack?"

There was an uncomfortable silence. Anne saw Jack's jaw tense and knew he wasn't happy about her being so direct, so she tried to keep her focus on Georgie.

"Yes, do tell us. It seems so many years ago that I've quite forgotten how it started," Barbara said.

Georgie sipped her wine and then sighed as if she was answering a question she had been asked a hundred times before. "It began the year before Mum died. She had cancer and knew she wasn't going to last long. She was desperate to find out what had happened to Jack."

"Did you know I existed before that?" Jack asked.

"No, we didn't. Mum had never mentioned you," Georgie said. Seeing the pained expression on Anne's face, she quickly added, "It wasn't because she didn't love you or didn't think about you. She was ashamed of what she had done, and that's why she kept it hidden all those years. Telling me about you was a great relief to her. My regret is that I couldn't locate you before she died."

"When she told you about me, did she explain how we got separated?" Jack said.

"Of course. It was the first question I asked her,"

Georgie said. "She had trouble talking about it, but eventually I got the whole sordid story."

"Sordid?" Jack said.

"That's my word, not hers. Although whenever I think about Andrew McPherson, it fits," Georgie said.

"Her husband. Our father," said Jack.

"He was indeed, though he never would have believed Harry and I were his children."

"Are you saying McPherson thought she was pregnant by another man?"

"He didn't know she was pregnant when she left. She was too afraid to tell him."

"Moira said nothing about him not knowing."

"It isn't something I've ever discussed with anyone outside this room. It was my mother's wee secret and she wanted to keep it that way."

"Moira told us that McPherson beat her."

"Moira told you? You didn't know already?" Georgie asked.

"I have little memory of those years."

"Well, it's true enough. Mum said he beat her like a drum—every Saturday night after the pub and sometimes on Sunday for good measure. He never hit her around the head, but the rest of her body was always bruised. In the Gorbals in those days, no one thought twice about a man strapping his wife. All she could do was put up with it or leave him. Then she met a neighbour, a widower, and they became friends."

"You mean they were lovers?" Jack asked.

"No, she swears they were just friends. He liked the lads more than the lassies," Georgie said. "But they were affectionate with each other, and one day McPherson caught them having a cuddle outside the house. He went crazy. He screamed at them, calling her a whore. He broke her friend's nose and kicked him after he fell to the ground. Then he dragged her into the house by the hair and belted her so badly she couldn't go outside for days. Shortly after that she realized she was pregnant."

"What a horrible situation," Anne said.

"An abortion wasn't an option. Even if it had been, she was a staunch Roman Catholic," Georgie said. "So she had only two choices — tell McPherson about the pregnancy or leave. The problem with telling him was that she was convinced he would believe her friend was the father. She could imagine McPherson attacking him again, and she was sure he'd beat her senseless or, even worse, she thought he might kill her. So she left."

Jack lowered his head and stared at his empty whisky glass. The room was so quiet that Anne could hear the clock on the mantel ticking.

"I think some of you could use a refill," Harry said. "Any takers?"

"Yes, I'll have another," Jack said and held up his glass.

"I'll wait," Anne said.

"Me too," said Georgie.

"It's a right sad story," Barbara said as Harry went to

the buffet. "It's difficult in this day and age to accept that life back then was so hard for so many women."

"It is sad, I grant you, and I certainly don't blame her for leaving him," Jack said. "But I still don't understand why she decided to abandon me."

Harry stood next to Jack with a refilled glass in his hand. Jack took the drink from him and looked across the coffee table at Georgie. "What did she tell you about leaving me?"

Georgie shook her head. "You're confusing me."

"I'm simply trying to understand her side of the story. What did she say happened?"

"She said she left you with McPherson."

"She told you that?"

"Yes. She said you were his favourite. She thought that if she left you with him, he wouldn't come after her."

"That's the same story she told Moira," Jack said.

"Is it not what happened?" Harry asked.

"She took Moira and me to the movies. After the first feature, she and Moira went to the toilet. They never came back. She didn't leave me with McPherson. She left me sitting by myself in the theatre," Jack said. "When the cleaners discovered me after the second feature, I was taken to the manager's office. Questions were asked. Answers were given. Phone calls were made. Finally a nun appeared. She told me they didn't know where my mother was. I remember telling her I wanted to go home. She said they had talked to my father and he didn't want me. So she took me to St. Martha's Orphanage."

"Did the orphanage try to contact Jessie?" Barbara asked, her voice breaking.

"I don't know. All I know is that during the six months I was there, neither she nor my father made an appearance."

"How did you end up in America?" Harry asked.

"One of the nuns was American. She had a brother who lived near Boston. He and his wife were childless and eager to adopt. They took me in when no one else wanted me, and I took their name."

"I don't know," Georgie muttered.

"You don't know what?" Anne said.

"I'm sorry. I'm confused," said Georgie.

"About what?" Anne pressed.

"Jack's story about Mum. I can't imagine her abandoning her own wee son in a cinema," she said, and then looked at Harry. "Do you think Mum was capable of such a thing?"

He shook his head. "I don't know what to think."

"Are you suggesting I invented this?" Jack asked.

"No, but it was more than fifty years ago and you were very young. Time has a way of playing tricks on the memory, and you did say you can't remember much from your early years."

"There's nothing wrong with my memories about that specific day," Jack said.

"Your mother was under tremendous stress when she left your father. Do you think it's possible that her memory was the faulty one?" Anne asked. "Or maybe she was in denial about what she had done and created an alternative history as a way of coping."

"She wasn't a woman to tell lies," Georgie said.

"She may not have considered it a lie. She may have convinced herself that her version of events was true, to avoid feeling guilty."

"Her memories were painful but she spoke about them openly. I don't know why she wouldn't be as honest about Jack," said Georgie.

"Maybe she was being open about the things done *to* her, rather than things done by her."

"You didn't know her."

"That's true. I'm simply trying to understand," Anne said.

"All I know is that Mum wouldn't hurt a fly, let alone her own son," Georgie said.

"She was estranged from Moira, though, wasn't she?" Jack asked.

"Moira is difficult. Mum wasn't the only person she didn't get along with," Georgie said. "What did you think of her?"

Jack hesitated and then shrugged. "Truthfully, she isn't someone I want to spend more time with."

"That reflects how Harry and I feel about her."

"All the same, perhaps Moira reminded your mother of her life with McPherson, while you and Harry represented her new life with a new husband," Jack said. "By the way, Moira did say nice things about both of you, and about the man your mother married—what was his name, Davey Montgomery?"

"He wasn't a saint, but he treated her well and he was kind to us," Harry said.

"Speaking of Davey, roast beef was his favourite dinner, and that's what I've prepared tonight," Barbara said. She looked at the coffee table. "No one has touched the cheese and crackers, so you should have plenty of room."

"Thanks, Barbara. That was a timely change of subject," Harry said, eyeing his watch. "Why don't we move into the dining room."

"Yes. And while we eat I'd like to hear all about your children," Barbara said.

Everyone stood up.

"I need to go to the loo," Georgie said to Jack and Anne. "It's upstairs, in case you need it."

"And we have some work to do in the kitchen," Barbara said. "Go on through to the dining room, and take your drinks with you."

Jack and Anne followed Harry and Barbara down the hall and turned left into the dining room. The table was set for six. Jack and Anne sat together, facing the door.

"Georgie is very defensive about her mother," Anne whispered. "Don't push too hard."

"The woman wouldn't hurt a fly? What a joke."

"Jack, please."

He nodded, but she wasn't sure what that meant.

14

GEORGIE WAS UPSTAIRS FOR quite some time, and Anne wondered if she was gathering herself. Her delight at meeting her long-lost brother had disappeared when they were discussing Jessie. Anne hoped both Georgie and Jack would be calmer over dinner.

When Georgie finally entered the dining room, Harry and Barbara followed, carrying a large green salad and two bottles of red wine. "I'm letting the beef rest, so we'll start with this," Harry said.

The conversation idled as the salad and wine were served. Anne was grateful for the distraction. All the talk about Jessie McPherson had exposed raw feelings, and it was clear that Jack and Georgie had different memories of the same woman. There was no right or wrong; there was just different.

As the meal progressed, Anne saw Georgie and Jack exchanging glances while Harry anxiously kept a watchful eye on both of them. She sensed this hadn't turned out the way he had wanted, and that he was looking for a way to broker a peace. She tried to help by saying to Barbara, "Tell us about your children. Harry said they're at school in England."

Barbara smiled. "Alastair is in his final year of architecture at the University of Sheffield, and Ellen is in second-year medicine at the University of Leicester. I don't know why they both felt the need to go to England to study, but it seems to have worked out well for them. Not only are they at excellent universities, they've also met partners there."

"Both of whom are English," Harry added.

"Is that still a problem? I understand that the English and Scots have a history of animosity, but I assumed that was all in the past."

"It's better than it used to be, but there are still flare-ups, usually when the English try to run roughshod over us," said Harry. "On a personal level, though, there's no animosity. Alastair's and Ellen's partners are lovely people."

"And your daughter, Elizabeth?" Anne asked Georgie. "Harry said she has ambitions of becoming an actress. How is she pursuing her dreams?"

"She's pursuing them here in Scotland. She just graduated from the Glasgow College of Dramatic Art. Who knows where that will lead? It's a hard industry to get a foothold in."

"What kind of work has she done?"

"She's been in some college productions, was an extra in a few films, and has done some local television adverts."

"We have a son-in-law in the film business in Los Angeles. If Elizabeth ever wanted to talk to him, I'm sure he'd be pleased to accommodate her," Anne said.

Georgie's eyes wavered, and Anne realized she was a bit tipsy. "That would be grand of him," Georgie said. "Education and raw talent are fine, but without contacts, without someone to give you a leg up, it's difficult to get ahead. And by the way, we call her Liz, not Elizabeth. I should have said that earlier."

"How about your children?" Barbara asked Anne. "What are they up to?"

"Well, Allison, our oldest, is married to Tony—he's the one in the film business. They have one son and Allison is at home looking after him. Mark is a commodities trader in Chicago and he's unmarried. Brent is a banker in New York. He and his wife Maggie have a baby daughter."

Harry started to pour wine before realizing both bottles were empty. He went to the kitchen and came back with two more. "I have something stronger if anyone wants it," he said.

"The wine will be fine for me," Jack said.

He had hardly spoken since they sat down, and now all eyes were drawn to him.

"How did you get to be so successful?" Georgie asked him, slurring her *s*'s.

Jack shrugged. "I was in the right place at the right time."

"Don't be so modest."

"I'm not being modest. I had a solid education in accounting and I love to work, but there were other factors that took me to the top," he said. "When I started at Pilgrim, it was a second-class insurance company that didn't attract the best talent. I was the first Bentley graduate to join the firm."

"Bentley, I take it, is a prestigious accounting school."

"It is. So when I joined Pilgrim, I was immediately earmarked as an up-and-comer. On top of that, most of the senior management team were in their late sixties. They started retiring almost as soon as I joined the firm, which meant I was able to move up quickly. Promotion through attrition."

"That's a silly thing to say, Jack," Anne interjected as Harry went around the table with fresh wine.

"Why's that?" Georgie asked.

"Jack worked night and day to make Pilgrim a success. He moulded it and willed it into becoming what it is today. I won't let him downplay his achievements."

"He created one of the great insurance companies of America," Harry said.

"Mum would be proud," Georgie added.

"I don't think I want to talk about her any more tonight," Jack said, and took a big sip of wine.

"I think that's best," Harry said.

"I don't," Georgie countered.

"Och, Georgie, come on," Barbara said, extending a hand towards her sister-in-law.

"Don't 'och, Georgie' me," Georgie said. "I don't want to cause a fuss, but I also don't want to leave things as they were before dinner. Jack was painting Mum as a villain, and that's not right."

"I never used the word *villain*. But tell me, after hearing what I had to say, how would you characterize her?"

"She was a victim. The real villain was Andrew McPherson. Why aren't you going after him? Why aren't you calling him to account?"

"How could I do that? The man is dead."

"Says who?"

"There's no record of him."

"You mean no record that you could find," she said.

"Do you mean to say he's alive?" asked Jack in disbelief.

Georgie nodded. "He was three years ago. I don't know about now."

"You never told me that," Harry said, looking stunned.

Georgie grimaced. "I didn't want to bother you with it. Besides, it came to nothing."

"How so?" Harry said.

"I went to a pub where I was told he was a regular, and I saw him there. But I didn't have the nerve to approach him," she said.

"What did he look like?" asked Jack.

"You would never guess the man is almost eighty. He

looked a bit seedy, but seemed fit, had a full head of grey hair, and wasn't excessively wrinkled."

"How big is he?" Jack asked.

"Medium height, medium build."

"What did you learn about him?" Jack said. "If you located him, you must have found out something about his life. Did he remarry? Did he have more kids?"

"What I learned was that he hadn't changed much since his days with our mother," she said.

"What do you mean?"

"I had tried to find him through channels like health and social services but failed. So I went back to the address Mum told me had been theirs. I talked to some of the older neighbours and they remembered him. One said that after Mum left, he went through several more women. When the war started, he joined the navy, but he came home to Glasgow and back to the house when it was over."

"Did he live by himself?" Jack asked.

"For a few years, but then he was sent to prison for killing a man in a pub fight. He was given ten years for it, and then while he was in prison he killed another man, so they added four more years to his sentence."

"How do you know this?" Barbara asked.

"The *Glasgow Standard* has a file on him. They referred to him as Douglas Andrew McPherson. Mum always called him Andrew, but it turns out that Andrew was his middle name. He reverted to Douglas when he got out of prison. I guess he hoped that would fool people."

"How did you find him?" Harry asked.

"One of his old neighbours said she'd seen him in a pub on Calvin Street, about half a mile from his old house. I went to that pub every afternoon for three days. He showed up on the third."

"How did you know it was him?"

"I had a photo from the *Standard* and I had the neighbour with me. She cost me two lagers a day, but it was worth it when she identified him."

"You said this was three years ago?" Jack asked.

"That's about right."

"You're certain it was him?"

"I had the photo and the neighbour."

"But you don't know if he's still alive."

"No, I don't."

"How could we find out?"

"I'm sure the pub is still there, and I still have his photo from the *Standard* if you want it."

"Why didn't you talk to him?" Jack asked.

"He scared me," Georgie said. "I remembered our mother's stories about him, and then I thought about him killing two men. He's old, but he still looked strong enough to beat me if he wanted. I know that was irrational, but I couldn't help thinking it."

"You did the right thing," Barbara said.

"I agree. There's enough danger in this world already without deliberately putting yourself in harm's way," Anne said.

Harry looked at Jack. "I'm shocked by all of this. I can't imagine how you feel. You came here to see Moira, and now . . ."

"I admit this is a lot to absorb," Jack said.

"He's probably dead by now," Georgie said.

"Even if he isn't, there's no reason to go looking for him," Anne said.

"That's true," said Jack.

Conversation lagged again as the facts of Douglas Andrew McPherson's life sunk in. Jack felt Anne's hand on his knee, and when he turned to her, she mouthed, *Maybe we should leave?*

"I have a fine old single malt, cognac, and Grand Marnier," Harry said loudly. "Who wants what?"

"You and Barbara have been wonderful hosts, but I think it's time we made our way back to the hotel," Jack said. "We're both a little jet-lagged and in need of a good night's sleep."

"But we'll see you tomorrow?" asked Harry.

"Of course."

"Barbara and I have to work, but our evening's free."

"The same for me," Georgie said.

"Then why don't you be our guests for dinner at the hotel tomorrow night," Jack said.

Harry looked at Georgie, and as one they said, "That would be perfect."

"I'll call you with the details," Jack said, rising from his chair.

"Great. Let me get my car keys and I'll take you back to the hotel."

"Harry, I think we should phone for a taxi. We've all had a lot to drink," Anne said.

"Nonsense, I can drive."

The group began to make their way to the front door. Barbara exchanged polite hugs with Jack and Anne. Georgie hung back, observing. But when Jack looked at her, she stepped forward and threw her arms around his neck. "I'm so happy we've found you," she said, her voice thick. "Let's not squabble about Mum anymore. Let's just celebrate the fact that we're finally together."

"I'm also glad we've connected," Jack said.

Georgie let go of him and smiled at Anne. "He's such a handsome man. According to our mum he was a beautiful wee boy. I have some old photos of him she left me, if you ever want to see them."

Anne saw Jack stiffen. "That would be lovely. Another time," she said.

15

GEORGIE AND BARBARA STOOD in the open doorway and waved as they got in the car.

"Georgie really surprised me," Harry said as he started down the street.

"How's that?" Jack asked.

"She never told me about McPherson."

"What would you have done if she had told you?" Anne asked.

"I don't think I would have done anything. Davey Montgomery was my father. McPherson doesn't mean anything to me," Harry said. "Unlike Georgie, I have no interest in revisiting the past."

"That's because your past has clarity," said Jack.

"Sorry. I wasn't implying that you shouldn't be pursuing yours."

"That's okay, I wasn't offended. Although, speaking of offence, I did seem to annoy Georgie quite a bit," Jack said.

"She's emotional at the best of times, and these aren't the best of times for her."

"I was going to ask her about her husband but decided it wasn't the right time for that," Jack said.

"That was thoughtful of you," Harry said. "But truthfully, where that's concerned, there'll never be a right time."

"That makes me even more curious," Jack said.

"Jack!" Anne said.

"No, that's okay," Harry said. "We are family, after all."

"Shouldn't it be left up to Georgie when and what to tell us about her husband?" Anne asked.

"Maybe I've been making more of an issue of it than I should. Besides, all you have to do is ask around the local financial community. You'll hear the stories about Atholl Malcolm soon enough."

"So he was involved in some financial shenanigans?" Jack asked.

"He claimed he lost the money he was managing through a series of bad investments. But if you ask the people who gave him their money to invest, they'll say he stole it. Some were willing to give him the benefit of the doubt, but he lost that when he buggered off."

"He took off?"

"He did what we call a midnight flit. Georgie got up one morning to find a note saying he'd left the country and would contact her as soon as he was settled. That was nine months ago. She hasn't heard from him since."

"Does she know where he is?" asked Jack.

"She swears she doesn't, and no one else seems to either."

"Why did she lose the house?"

"She's completely skint. Everything they owned was in either his name or his company's. The creditors went after it all. Georgie might have been able to hang on to some bits and pieces if she'd fought for them, but the way Atholl left took the fight right out of her."

"The poor woman," Anne said.

"What happened to the money?" Jack asked.

"The prevailing opinion is that he'd been stashing it overseas for years in some offshore haven. There's no proof, of course, but that doesn't end the speculation."

"What do you believe?"

"I'm not sure Atholl was smart enough or had the foresight to pull off something like that. I think it's just as likely that he did lose the money," Harry said. "Not that the investors care. All that matters is that it's gone."

"Has he been charged with anything?"

"Not yet, but I've heard the anti-fraud department is looking into it. Though that would be the least of his concerns. Word is the Baxter brothers are looking for him too."

"And they are?"

"Scottish criminal royalty—the Baxters are four brothers who run most of the drug and prostitution business in Glasgow and the surrounding towns. At one time their father had the biggest bookie operation in the country. Our stepfather, Davey Montgomery, worked for him years ago, and he stayed in touch with the family. It was Davey who got Atholl together with the brothers."

"Davey is dead, correct?"

"He died ages ago."

"Did Atholl and the brothers do business together for a long time?"

"They did, and he must have made them some money, because they kept investing with him. I've heard they may have lost as much as five million pounds when Atholl did his flit," Harry said. "If that's true, then it's hard to blame Atholl for leaving. The Baxters don't believe in lawyers, and *bankruptcy* isn't in their vocabulary."

"They would have harmed him?" Anne asked.

"Killed him, most likely."

"Good grief. No wonder Georgie is upset," Anne said. "Would they harm her?"

"No, but they've made it clear that if she hears from Atholl, she's to pass the information along to them."

"Would she?"

"It would be risky for her and Liz not to," said Harry.

The starkness of that admission caused the conversation to stall. Jack looked out the window onto quiet streets. Suddenly he felt quite far from Wellesley. "What kind of business did Atholl run?" he finally asked.

"Calling it a business is a bit of a stretch," Harry said. "He was a trader. He bought and sold anything he thought he could make a quid on. Cheese, clothes, fish, wine, televisions, tractors—you name it and he probably traded in it at some point. The problem was that the volumes he dealt in kept getting bigger, and that of course increased his exposure. One or two bad deals would really hurt him. One or two very bad deals would have killed his business."

"Is that what you think happened?"

"My theory is that he made a couple of bad deals and lost some serious money. Rather than trying to make it back, he took whatever was left and headed for the hills."

"That doesn't speak well of him."

"He was always a bit of a prick," Harry said, and then turned towards Anne. "Pardon my language."

"I've heard worse."

The illuminated clock tower of the North British Hotel appeared ahead of them. A moment later Harry parked in front of its entrance.

"Well, this was quite the day," Jack said.

"Wasn't it. I never would have guessed when I got out of bed this morning that my day would end like this."

"I feel the same."

"So, until tomorrow then," Harry said, extending his hand.

"Yes," Jack said, taking it.

Anne got out of the back seat and stood on the sidewalk. Harry climbed out of the car to say goodbye to her. "I'm so happy for Jack," she said.

"I'm happy for all of us."

After an exchange of hugs, Anne walked into the hotel with Jack trailing behind her. They didn't speak until they reached their suite and the door was closed behind them.

"What do you think about tonight?" she asked.

"I don't know."

"No?"

He shrugged. "Part of me is pleased. Part of me is confused. Part of me hurts."

"It isn't like you to be indecisive."

"There are just so many complications."

"Every family is complicated."

"True, but I had nothing to do with creating these particular complications."

"Are you talking about your father, about McPherson?"

"No, I meant what I said to Harry. I have no interest in the man."

"Atholl Malcolm?"

"Partially, but also Georgie."

"I feel sorry for Georgie."

"We hardly know her."

"Jack! I know she upset you when she defended your mother. All I can say is that I hope my children would do the same for me. You have to separate Georgie's feelings for her mother from your mother's behaviour towards you."

"There you go again, being entirely reasonable."

"Would you prefer it if I simply agreed with everything you said?"

"Of course I would," he said with a wan smile.

"That isn't going to happen, Jack,"

"I know," he said, and then glanced at his watch.

"Do you have somewhere to be?" she asked.

"No, but it isn't quite ten yet. The office in Boston is still open," he said. "Are you going to shower before we go to bed?"

"Of course."

"Would you mind if I checked in with the office while you do?"

"Jack, you can do whatever you wish while I'm in the shower. But when I'm finished, I don't want to see you on that phone."

16

JACK WAITED UNTIL THE bathroom door was closed before he called Pam.

"Mr. Anderson, what can I do for you?" she asked, sounding slightly surprised.

"I'd like the phone numbers for Don Arnold and Ross Goldsmith."

"Yes, sir," she said hesitantly. "Is there a problem?"

"No, I just want their numbers, thank you."

"Of course, sir," she said.

When he had the numbers, Jack stared at his notepad. Arnold was Pilgrim's chairman; he had been appointed to the board by a union pension fund that had a large holding in the company. He had supported many of Jack's initiatives, but the two of them had never really hit it off. Their relationship had even been contentious on occasion. There were times, in fact, when Jack felt Arnold didn't completely trust him.

Goldsmith, the vice-chairman, was an old-timer. A New England commercial banker, he had been appointed to the board when Bob Young was still CEO and had often been vocal in his support for Jack. He didn't have Arnold's weight with the board, but he was liked and respected. *He's the one to make my case,* Jack thought as he called Goldsmith.

He was routed from a receptionist to Goldsmith's personal secretary and then put through to the man himself.

"Jack, I thought you were taking a holiday in Scotland," Goldsmith said.

"I am on a holiday of sorts, but you know me — I find it hard to let go of the business. I've been staying in touch with the office through Pam."

"Has something happened?"

"Only in the most indirect way," Jack said. "I was reviewing our preliminary results for the last quarter and was pleasantly surprised by how good they are. We're setting records in terms of sales, growth, and profit, and the trends show no indication of slowing — unless, of course, we change our direction."

"I haven't seen those results yet," Goldsmith said carefully.

"They're still being finalized. The board should have them by week's end."

"Wonderful. I look forward to getting them," Goldsmith said. "But Jack, it isn't like you to call me out of the blue, even with such good news. Is something else going on?"

"Yes. I've been doing a lot of thinking while I've been over here, and I find myself becoming increasingly worried about the future of the company."

"You just told me we're setting records."

"We are, and I can see a clear path ahead for us to reach our goal of becoming one of the Big Three. But to get there we need to maintain our momentum. We need to keep going at full bore."

"What makes you think we won't keep up our momentum?"

Jack hesitated. This was the crucial moment, and he reminded himself to be calm and low-key. "Ross, we've known each other for many years and we've shared many confidences. But this is one that I need your absolute assurance will remain strictly between us."

"You have my assurance," Goldsmith said, after his own slight hesitation.

"Well, as difficult as this is for me to say, I've been having serious doubts about Norman Gordon's ability to run our company."

"What brought this on? Has something happened?"

"No, but he's made a number of comments that, taken together, give me concern," Jack said.

"In what way?"

"I've heard him say that the company needs to slow down, that we need to take some time to consolidate our gains. He's even talked about taking a few steps back," Jack said. "I find that worrying, even alarming. We've become a national brand by acting aggressively, and I don't want to see that aggression disappear just as we're about to crack the Big Three. Another two years or maybe three like the one we're having will get us there."

"Have you spoken to Norman about this?"

"I have. He understands my position and agrees with me in theory. But I think he's just paying me lip service."

"What are you trying to say?" Goldsmith asked.

"I'm not comfortable about turning the reins of the company over to Norman."

"He's been chosen. The decision has already been made."

"He could be unchosen."

"That would be messy," Goldsmith said. "And you know our board doesn't like messes."

"Another possibility would be to leave him in position as my successor but postpone the handover date," Jack said, as casually as he could.

"Ah," Goldsmith said. "The penny drops."

Jack didn't respond. He knew Goldsmith was thinking over his proposal, and the best thing for him to do was wait.

"Jack, are you suggesting that you remain as president and CEO until Norman is better prepared to take over?" Goldsmith finally said.

"I don't want to sound egotistical, but who is better positioned to maintain our rate of growth and take us to the next level?"

"No one, but that still doesn't mean it's a good idea."

"I know there would be challenges."

"That's an understatement. For one thing, you've already announced your resignation and set a date for your departure. For another, Norman has been publicly named as your successor. Reversing those actions would generate questions in the market, which could create uncertainty about the company. It would certainly seed doubts about Norman's capacity to lead."

"Those are things that a vigorous public relations program could overcome."

"Perhaps, but only if we provided a strong answer to the question everyone is sure to ask."

"Which is why is it necessary for me to stay on?"

"Exactly."

"The answer is that the company is in the middle of a five-year expansion plan that I began. The board has decided that, rather than handing it off to Norman, they want me to see it through to its conclusion."

"I wasn't aware that we had a five-year plan."

"We didn't call it that, but my strategy was plain enough."

"Okay, let's assume the board agrees that it would be beneficial for you to stay on. What do you propose we do about the Young resolution?"

"It would have to be overturned."

"You would ask the board to do that?"

"No, you know I couldn't. It wouldn't look right. The initiative would have to come from a board member, as would the request that I stay on as CEO."

"You want me to go to the board to persuade them to ask you to rescind your resignation?"

"I want you to do what you think is best for the company."

"You're smooth, Jack, I'll give you that," Goldsmith said.

"All I care about is doing the right thing for Pilgrim, the company I've devoted my entire working life to."

"I apologize — I was being glib. But you can understand that I feel blindsided by all this," Goldsmith said.

"Of course, and I apologize for that. This has been weighing on me for a while. It's only since I've been here, in a different environment, that I've begun to see things clearly."

"It's true that more than a few board members were unhappy when you resigned, and there wasn't much enthusiasm for Norman as your replacement," Goldsmith said slowly.

"Ross, I've made it clear to you that I want to stay on."

"Yes, you have."

"I want to finish what I've started. Will you support me? Will you speak to the board on my behalf?"

"This is not something you can just spring on them. Despite their admiration for you and their reservations about Norman, they might not react positively to a complete reversal of their plans. And the last thing you want is for the board to turn down the idea. It would be an unseemly end to an otherwise terrific career."

"I'm not suggesting you go directly to the board.

I understand there would have to be pre-consultation, a lot of one-on-one conversations. The board isn't scheduled to meet again until next month. That represents a window of opportunity."

"It does," Goldsmith said, and then paused. "Look, Jack, I'm not going to make a commitment to you now, but I agree that your proposal makes some sense. I'm prepared to make some discreet phone calls. I would like to gauge how my fellow board members might react if the idea were brought forward."

"I couldn't ask for more."

"When do you get back from Scotland?"

"Next week."

"I should have a reading by then. If it's positive, then we can talk about making a pitch to the board. If it isn't, I trust that you'll throw all your support behind Norman and make the transition as smooth as possible."

"You have my word on that."

"Then we'll talk when you get back."

"If something urgent comes up in the interim, I can be reached at the North British Hotel in Edinburgh. If there's a change in my situation, I'll let Pam know."

Jack put the phone back in its cradle, feeling pleased with the way the conversation had gone. He trusted Goldsmith. He was sure the banker would make the phone calls and would never mention that Jack had initiated the idea.

Talking to Goldsmith had restored Jack's sense of normalcy. Corporate matters, even corporate intrigues, were his natural element. The past two days, and particularly the evening with Georgie, had taken him out of his comfort zone. *Thank God Anne was there tonight*, he thought. If she hadn't been there to soften some of Georgie's opinions about their mother, he wasn't sure how he would have reacted. How could Georgie not understand how he felt? How could she not believe he had been abandoned? Harry seemed to have a better sense of things, but maybe he just thought it was better to keep quiet.

He heard Anne moving about in the bedroom and went to the open door. "It's mid-afternoon in California if you want to call Allison," he said.

"Do you think I should?" she asked, as she put her hairbrush into a toilet case.

"There's a lot to tell her."

"But you know what's she like," Anne said. "She'll be quick to pass on the news to the other kids. Are you prepared for an avalanche of congratulations when you're not sure yet how you feel about all this?"

"You're right. Maybe we should hold off."

Anne yawned. "Besides, I'm tired. Between the wine, the jet lag, and all the emotional turmoil, I'm quite done in."

"Me too. What would you like to do tomorrow?"

"We can't come to Edinburgh and not see the castle."

"The castle it is, then."

17

LIGHT WAS PEEKING THROUGH the curtains when Jack awoke, alone in the bed. That surprised him because Anne was rarely the first one up. He went to the bathroom to brush his teeth. When he entered the living room, Anne was sitting on the sofa in front of a tray on the coffee table.

"I can't remember the last time you slept this late. It's already past nine," she said, and motioned to the tray. "I ordered a large pot of coffee. It's still hot."

"How did you sleep?" he asked as he poured himself a cup.

"Really well."

"I didn't. I started off thinking about work and then found myself fixating on Georgie and our mother. The last thing I thought about before going to sleep was McPherson. I don't know why he was in my head, but he was."

"I'm not surprised to hear that. You were a bit casual

about him last night, but he's another unresolved issue. You've seen your mother's grave; maybe you need to see his too—assuming that he's dead."

"I could go to the health service in Glasgow and make enquiries, but I don't know if they'll have any answers for me," he said. "It might be better to go to the pub Georgie mentioned and ask about him there."

"So we'd go to Glasgow?"

"It's only an hour away."

"You'll have to contact Georgie if you want the photo."

"I'll call Harry."

"Before you do, let's decide where we're going to have dinner tonight," Anne said. "I've been looking through this Edinburgh guide, and it has a list of the best restaurants in the city. The hotel isn't mentioned, but there's one called Bannockburn further along Princes Street that's highly recommended."

"I'll ask the concierge to make a reservation," Jack said as he walked over to the desk, where his blazer hung on the back of the chair. He reached into a pocket and took out the slip of paper with Caledonia Insurance's phone number. He dialled, then said, "Mr. Harry Montgomery, please. Tell him that Jack Anderson is calling."

"Jack, good morning. It's good to hear from you. I hope you and Anne had a comfortable night's sleep."

"It was fine, Harry, thanks for asking," Jack said. "We were thinking about going to the Bannockburn tonight rather than eat at the hotel. Does that suit you?"

"Indeed. It's one of the best in the city."

"Seven o'clock?"

"Perfect."

"Also I'd like to get in touch with Georgie."

"Certainly . . ." Harry said hesitantly. "But I can let her know about dinner if that's the reason."

"Actually, I've decided that I want to know more about McPherson after all. I thought I'd go to that pub in Glasgow and do some poking around. She has the information I need to get started."

"I see. Give me a second," Harry said. The second turned into a minute before he returned. "Sorry, Jack, I was just checking to see if she was working today. She isn't, so you should be able to reach her at home. Here's the number."

"Thanks. And we're looking forward to seeing you and Barbara tonight," Jack said.

He put down the phone and walked over to the sofa. "Would you mind calling Georgie?" he said to Anne. "You seemed to get along well, so the request might be easier coming from you. All I need is the name of the pub, some general idea of where it is, and the photo from the newspaper."

"I suspect this is less about how Georgie and I got along and more about your not wanting to answer any questions about why you want to look for him," Anne said.

"Yes, I admit that's part of it."

Anne shook her head. "Give me the number."

She went to the desk and dialled. Jack poured himself another coffee and watched her intently.

"Georgie, good morning. This is Anne," she began, and after a few more general pleasantries she said, "We've decided to try to find out what happened to Douglas Andrew McPherson. Since we're here in Scotland, why not take advantage of it? We would appreciate it if you could give us the name of the pub where you saw him and if you could lend us that newspaper photo."

Anne listened for a moment and then said, "You don't have to do that." Then, after a longer pause, "We'll see you here, then. Call us when you get to the lobby."

"What did she say?" Jack asked when Anne had hung up.

"Georgie insists on coming with us. She'll be here around noon with the address and the photo."

"I'm not sure I like that idea."

"I do," she said. "She'll know where to go and she'll recognize him if he's there."

"That's assuming he's still alive. I can't help hoping he's not."

"Why do you feel that way?"

"It's much easier to deal with the idea of him in the abstract. I'm not sure how I'll feel if he's alive."

"Let's hope you don't have to find out. But if he is alive, having Georgie along will give you someone else to share that burden. Besides, whether he's alive or dead, the people at the pub may be more inclined to speak to a local than American tourists."

"That is true."

Anne looked at her watch. "We have a couple of hours to kill before noon. If you get dressed right now we should have time to take a castle tour. It lasts about two hours."

"Let's do that," he said.

Twenty minutes later they left the hotel for the ten-minute walk to the castle. It stood on Castle Rock, overlooking the city, and was a formidable sight. Jack hadn't been overly impressed by anything he'd seen during their Burns tour in Ayrshire, but the castle made an impact. He keenly took in thousand-year-old St. Margaret's Chapel and the Great Hall, and he enjoyed the guide's stories about the sieges the castle had withstood. He respected perseverance, and to suffer through twenty-six sieges in a thousand years—including the "Lang Siege," which lasted two years—embodied it.

At ten to twelve they walked back to the hotel to find Georgie, wearing blue jeans and a red fleece sweater, waiting for them in the lobby. "I hope we didn't keep you waiting," Anne said after a hug. "We did the castle tour."

"I just got here a few minutes ago. The bus was punctual for once."

"Did you speak to Harry this morning?" Jack asked.

"Yes, and I told him I'm going with you."

"How did he react?"

"He didn't seem to care one way or another, but with Harry you can never really tell what's he's thinking." She smiled. "As you've seen, I'm the opposite."

"Did he tell you about dinner?"

"He mentioned the Bannockburn. It's a great restaurant."

"It was Anne's choice. And speaking of food, do you think we should have some lunch before we head out?" he asked.

"I could use some lunch, but why not pub food? The Tartan Rover has traditional fare, if you can handle sausage rolls, Scotch eggs, and meat pies."

"Is that the pub in Glasgow?"

"It is."

"That sounds like a good idea to me," Anne said.

"Then I'll ask them to bring the car around and we'll hit the road," said Jack.

Anne and Georgie went to the hotel entrance while Jack spoke to the front desk. When he rejoined them, Anne was holding a photo. "I hope you don't mind, but I asked Georgie to show me the picture," Anne said.

Jack reached for it.

"It's rather uncanny, don't you think?" Anne said. "It gave me a bit of a jolt."

Jack looked at the photo and blinked. It was grainy and some of McPherson's features were blurred, but his square chin, wide brow, and thick hair were plain enough. "When was this taken?" he asked Georgie.

"Close to thirty years ago."

"He would have been close to the age I am now."

"We all have that chin and brow," Georgie said.

"Thank goodness that's all you inherited from him," Anne said as Jack passed the photo back to Georgie.

"I'll show you some photos of Mum . . . when you're ready. None of us look much like her," she said.

Jack didn't answer, and when the car arrived, that topic of conversation ended. "Since Georgie is our guide, it might be easier if she sat in front with me," Jack said to Anne.

"That's fine," she said.

Traffic was light when they exited the city. As they sped down the highway towards Glasgow, Anne asked questions about Liz and answered Georgie's about her own children. When they reached Glasgow, Georgie focused on their route, pointing out landmarks.

"You know the city very well," Jack said.

"I lived here for a while and then in Bearsden, a small town nearby, for years. I used to come into the city all the time for shopping and the like."

"Are you firmly settled in Edinburgh now?" Anne said.

"I don't know about settled, but I have a nice apartment and a decent job that I can walk to."

"Where are you working?" Jack asked.

"I'm a salesclerk in the Goldbergs department store near Tollcross," she said, and then added quickly, "You should start looking for a place to park. We're getting close to the pub."

The Tartan Rover came into view a few hundred yards later. Jack pulled into a public parking lot almost directly across from it. "How do you think we should handle this?" he asked Georgie after he'd turned off the engine.

"We'll have lunch. That will give us a chance to have a look around and get acclimatized. Also, the pub staff might be more co-operative if we've spent some money."

"Then let's go and eat," he said.

From the outside, the pub wasn't particularly inviting. It had a brown brick façade that was black in places, and small, dirty windows on either side of a glass door etched with thistles. The Tartan Rover sign above the door looked as if it had been hand-painted. Georgie saw the look on Jack's face and said, "The local pubs don't care much about outward appearances, but it will be better inside. And you don't have to worry about the food. They don't actually cook anything on the premises; all they do is heat up the pies and rolls they buy from bakers."

"If you say so," Jack said, as he opened the door for the women and was immediately hit by the smell of cigarette smoke.

At the furthest end from the door, the pub had a semicircular bar with eight stools. Padded benches in red leather were set against the walls, with rectangular wooden tables in front of them. About a dozen round tables with four chairs each had been squeezed into the remaining space. The grey walls were covered in plaques, each depicting a different clan tartan. At least half the tables were taken.

"We should sit against that wall. It will give us a good

view of the room and the door," Georgie said. They went over to the bench she'd indicated and sat side by side. The three of them at once scanned the room, looking for a familiar face. "I don't see him," said Georgie.

"I would have been shocked if you had," Jack said.

"Where are the menus?" Anne asked.

"The menu is on that blackboard," Georgie said, pointing just left of the bar. "And our orders will be taken at the bar. There's no table service here."

"What do you recommend?" asked Anne.

"You can't go far wrong with Scotch pies."

"I'll have that, then, with a glass of white wine."

"Do you drink beer?"

"Not often, but I can."

"I suggest you do so here. Maybe a lager?"

"That will be fine."

"Jack, how about you?" Georgie asked.

"I'll have the same."

"I'll be back," Georgie said, and got up and went over to the bar.

"This is certainly different. I can't remember the last time I was in a place where nearly everyone was smoking," Anne said.

"Or drinking so early in the afternoon."

They lapsed into silence as Georgie approached the table, gingerly balancing three pints of lager. She distributed the drinks, then raised hers. "Here's to good health and a long life," she said.

"Amen to that," said Anne.

Georgie sipped her beer, then turned towards Anne. "I spoke to Harry last night after dinner. I was saying how fortunate Jack is to have such a supportive spouse."

"That's a very nice thing to say."

"I mean it, and Harry agrees with me. But then of course he would, because Barbara is a rock for him."

"Barbara is lovely," Anne said, sensing that the conversation could be heading towards Atholl Malcolm.

"Harry told us a little about your husband," Jack said. "It sounds like you've had a rough go of things."

"What did he tell you?"

"He said Atholl ran into some financial difficulties and left the country."

Anne glared at him, angry that he had raised a topic that should have been Georgie's choice to initiate. "Jack, the relationship between Georgie and her husband is their business. We shouldn't be prying."

"I appreciate that, Anne," Georgie said, and then shrugged. "But it isn't something that can be ignored, and I'm finally at a point where I don't mind talking about it."

"You don't need to," Anne said.

"I know, but why not?"

"As long as you're comfortable doing it," Anne said.

Georgie shrugged again. "The truth is, Liz and I went from a very comfortable life to scraping for every pound and worrying about every penny. It has taken some getting used to, but we're getting there. The hardest thing for me isn't going without the things I used to take for granted. It's trying not to be consumed with rage at what that bastard did to us," she said in a rush.

"Harry implied that he left you high and dry," said Jack.

"'High and dry' is a nice way of putting it. What he did was take all the shit in his life, dump it on us, and then bugger off, leaving us to deal with the aftermath. And there seemed to be no end to it. The cars were repossessed, taken from our driveway in broad daylight so the neighbours could get a good view. Our bank account was frozen, even though he hadn't left much in it. Our credit cards were rejected at places where we used to be treated like royalty; and then, as if rejection wasn't enough, we'd be asked to hand over the cards to be destroyed. The bank started foreclosure on the house, but before they'd got far, some of his creditors came after us themselves. I just walked away from it."

"Was Liz living at home when this was going on?" Anne asked.

"No, she was at uni here in Glasgow, but it caught up to her when the cheque to cover her fees bounced and her credit cards became useless."

"How terrible! Did she manage to finish her school year?"

"Harry stepped in to help. I don't know what we would have done without him."

"That was good of him."

"He's a good man, unlike the bastard I married," she

said, then lifted the glass to her lips and took a deep swig. She wiped her mouth with the back of her hand and pointed at the bar. "I think the barman is telling us the pies are ready."

"I'll get them with you," Anne said.

As they walked to the bar, Anne saw there were only two other women in the pub, and both of them looked to be well past retirement age. "I'm sorry Jack raised the subject of your husband," Anne said softly.

"There isn't any right or wrong way to do it, so no apology is necessary," Georgie said.

"Another round?" the barman asked.

"I think we're set for now," Georgie said, and pointed at the pies. "Those look good."

Anne eyed the small, round pies sitting on paper plates, each surrounded by a clump of potato chips and a few bread-and-butter pickles. If they hadn't been on a mission, she might have passed on lunch.

Georgie took three sets of plastic cutlery wrapped in paper napkins from a container on the bar, picked up two of the pies, and headed back to the table, with Anne and her plate close behind.

The pies were encased in a pale brown crust. The sides and top were soft, more white than brown, while the circular rim was hard and dark. Georgie cut her pie from top to bottom into four equal portions. Inside was a brown minced meat that gave off a pleasant aroma. Jack and Anne followed Georgie's lead, and soon all three of them were eating.

"That tasted better than it looked," Jack said when he was done.

"Glad you enjoyed it," Georgie said, washing down her last bite with some lager.

They sat back and looked around the pub.

"When should we ask about McPherson?" Anne asked.

"Let's give it a few more minutes," Georgie said.

Jack had eaten everything on his plate, and now he reached for the chips that Anne hadn't touched. "Did you move to Edinburgh to be closer to Harry and Barbara?" he asked.

Georgie nodded. "Edinburgh is less than thirty miles from Bearsden, but for me it was like moving to another planet."

"I assume that was a positive thing."

"Definitely. I might have survived in Bearsden if it was just about losing material things, but I couldn't cope with the humiliation. People who I thought were friends stopped talking to me. They wouldn't take my phone calls, and if they saw me on the street they'd cross over to the other side to avoid me. If I accidently bumped into them in the shops, they couldn't look me in the eye, and several of them wouldn't speak to me at all."

"But surely people understood that you weren't to blame for your husband's actions," Anne said.

"People didn't differentiate. Liz and I were lumped in with him," she said. "I didn't know at the time, but I soon learned he had taken money from many of my friends to invest, and they looked at the way we lived as the ill-gotten fruit of their labours. The final straw came when Liz was home from uni to visit her old chums. I thought she'd be gone for the afternoon, but she was back in tears in less than an hour. She'd been wearing designer jeans, and one of the girls taunted her about them. She told Liz the entire town hated us and that if we were going to stay we should stop parading around in clothes that had been bought with stolen money."

"That's so cruel," Anne said.

"Aye, it was. I called Harry that night, and the next day Liz and I left for Edinburgh. I got the job at Goldbergs and Liz waits tables at a decent restaurant in between auditions. Things have improved. We don't have a lot of money but no one knows who we are, so memory of the shame and humiliation is starting to fade. Now all I have to deal with is my anger at Atholl."

"Harry mentioned something about the Baxter brothers. Have they been a problem?" asked Jack.

Georgie raised an eyebrow. "You said Harry told you a little about Atholl. It seems to me he told you a lot more than that."

"Only in passing. There wasn't a lot of detail."

She emptied her glass. "The Baxter family are thieves, pimps, and drug-dealers. Atholl was stupid to take their money in the first place and then an absolute fool to lose it. I believe they're the main reason why he left the way he did. He wouldn't have cared what anyone in Bearsden thought, but he was petrified of the Baxter boys coming after him. And come after him they would."

"Have they bothered you?"

"A couple of them paid me a visit shortly after he disappeared. I was in a fragile state that day, and I think they believed me when I told them I had no idea where he was," she said. "I thought I'd seen the last of them when I moved to Edinburgh, but even though they don't do much business there, one of their wives spotted me at Goldbergs and I received another wee visit. When they saw where I was living, they didn't doubt that he'd left me skint. One of them — his name is Billy, he's the youngest — slipped me two hundred pounds and said he'd give me ten times that if I was ever in a position to tell them where Atholl is. When I said I would if I got the chance, he put a tight grip on my arm and told me that if I knew something and didn't pass it along, they'd make sure I had a long stay in hospital."

Anne gasped. "Do you think he meant that?"

"Aye, I do."

"Do you have any idea where Atholl might be?" Jack asked.

"Are you joking?" Georgie snapped. "Believe me, if I found out tomorrow morning, Billy Baxter would know by tomorrow afternoon."

"I can't imagine hating someone that much. But then I haven't gone through anything like you've experienced," Anne said.

Georgie lowered her head. "We all have our trials. I've come to believe that what they are is less important than how we respond to them. I'm trying to make a good life for Liz and myself, and hopefully one day I'll get there. When I do, perhaps I can let go of the hate and be able to accept that Atholl was just a weak man caught up in circumstances he couldn't face."

"Like Jack's mother?" Anne asked.

"My mother was nothing like Atholl."

"Of course not, but her life was difficult, and maybe she didn't cope as well as she could have."

Georgie lifted her head and stared at Jack. "I feel so sad about what happened to you as a wee boy," she said. "But tell me honestly, knowing what you know now, do you hate our mother?"

He stared back at her, surprised by the question. "I'm not sure how to answer that," he said finally. "I have all these conflicting emotions that I'm trying to sort out. But I can tell you this: I'm very glad to have found you and Harry."

"That's so nice to hear."

There was an awkward silence, which Anne broke by saying, "Is it time to ask about McPherson?"

"Sure, let's do that," Georgie said, sliding off the bench.

They walked over to the bar. "I'll take the bill, please," Jack said to the barman.

"You sound like a Yank," the barman said.

"We're from Boston."

"We don't get many Yanks in here. Thanks for coming. Hope you enjoyed your meat pies."

"We did," Jack said as he pulled out his wallet.

The barman passed him the bill. Jack glanced at it, took twenty pounds from his wallet, and put it on top. "Keep the change."

"Thank you. That's right generous."

"We have something to ask you, though," Georgie said, taking the photo from her purse. "Do you recognize this man? He may have been a customer. His name is—"

"He looks like Dougie McPherson, only younger," the man interrupted.

"It's an old photo."

The barman took a closer look. "Aye, that's him. What do you want with Dougie?"

"We're related to him. He hasn't been in touch for ages, and our family would be happy to know he's alive. If that's actually what you're telling us—that he's alive."

"He is indeed."

"Does he still come here?"

"He does."

"When?"

"He's in most days, usually around six."

"How long does he stay?"

"Until last orders. Dougie is a hardy old soul."

"Will he be here tonight?"

"I doubt it. He was here the last two nights."

"So, tomorrow then?"

"Possibly."

"Do you know where he lives?" Jack asked.

"No more than I know where you live," the barman said.

"Well, could you do us a favour?" Jack said, reaching into his wallet. "Here's another twenty pounds. Could you call us the next time Dougie comes in? And I'll give you another forty pounds if you keep this between us."

"That's a strange request."

"We want to surprise him — in the nicest way imaginable, of course."

"I guess that would be all right," the barman said, taking the twenty.

"We're staying at the North British Hotel in Edinburgh. Do I need to give you the number?"

"No."

"And my name is Jack Anderson. If by some chance I'm not there when you call, leave a message."

"Another forty pounds, you said?"

"Yes, but only if we find him here. If he's gone, then no extra money."

"I understand."

"Okay, I think we're on the same page," Jack said, and turned to Anne and Georgie. "We can leave now."

They were no more than ten yards from the pub when Georgie came to an abrupt halt. Her hands were shaking. "I don't know how I held myself together in there," she said. "I didn't believe the man could still be alive."

"I'm stunned as well," Jack said.

"You don't look it."

"I've spent more than thirty years developing a calm veneer for business. Believe me, my emotions are running high."

"What are you going to do?" Anne asked.

"What do you mean?"

"Are you really going to meet with the man, to talk to him?"

"Why not?"

"Why would you is a more appropriate question," Georgie said. "What's to be gained?"

"Let's go to the car," Jack said, and started off in the direction of the parking lot.

"That's a fine way to answer," Georgie said to Anne as they looked at Jack's retreating back.

"He might not have an answer to give you," Anne said.

18

GEORGIE SAT IN THE front again on the drive back to Edinburgh. She was quiet until they reached the motorway. Then, as the car revved up to sixty miles an hour, she leaned over and touched Jack lightly on the arm. "I'm sorry if I sounded like a know-all back there," she said. "I shouldn't assume that you feel the same way I do about the man."

"He spooks you, doesn't he," Jack said.

"I thought I made that clear last night."

"Then why did you volunteer to come with us today? We could have done it without you."

"I thought I'd feel different if you and Anne were with me."

"Safety in numbers?"

"Precisely. But the second I heard he was alive, I felt the same anxiety I experienced when I saw him three years ago. I should never have gone there."

"He's not going to harm you. I would never let him do that."

"There are more ways to harm someone than belting them. Some people have a knack for worming their way into your head. They can sense where you're vulnerable and they attack your confidence, rip down your feelings of self-worth."

"You're ascribing a lot to a man you've never met."

"Mum talked about him in the months before she died," Georgie said, her brow furrowing. "She hadn't seen him in forty years, but he was still in her head."

"What did she say?" Anne asked softly.

"She said he was evil, a real Jekyll and Hyde. One minute all smiles and charm and the next a monster. She cried when she was describing how he would torment her. It always started with teasing. After a while she knew where that was going to lead, but she never figured out how to stop it. If she tried to humour him, the teasing become crueller until it was unbearable. If she tried to ignore him, the pretense would stop and he'd immediately turn to violence. The result was always the same. He'd rape her and then he'd beat her, accusing her of being an unfit wife, a foul person. He destroyed whatever self-esteem she had," Georgie said, and turned to look at Anne. "And I don't think she ever recovered it. She was a wee frightened mouse her entire life. Thank God Davey Montgomery came along and saved her."

"That poor woman. No one deserves to be treated like that," Anne said.

"Has Harry heard these stories?" Jack asked.

"They're not stories," Georgie said. "That was her life."

"I apologize. I wasn't trying to minimize what happened to her," Jack said. "I just wanted to know if she confided in Harry as well."

"No, I don't think she did, and I didn't either," Georgie said. "It was between Mum and me."

"What do you know about the man McPherson killed in the pub?" Jack asked.

"Just what I read in the *Standard*. The other man was a plumber who was in the pub for a drink after work. He and McPherson got into some kind of argument over unions. It led to punches, and then McPherson stuck a knife into the man's belly. The witnesses quoted in the paper said McPherson threw the first punch. The knife was his, of course."

"What about the man he killed in jail?"

"I don't know any details."

"And we don't need any," Anne said.

"I agree. McPherson seems like a nasty piece of work," Jack said.

Anne leaned forward until her mouth was next to Jack's ear. "I don't want you to go back to that pub. There's no need for it."

"He's an old man," Jack said.

"He's a vicious old man. I don't want you to go."

"I'm no threat to him. Neither are Georgie and Harry, for that matter."

"You never know."

"I won't make any promises. I need to think about it," he said, then glanced at his watch and looked at Georgie. "We still have a few hours before dinner. Do you have any plans for the rest of the afternoon?"

"I'll go home and change. Jeans and this old sweater won't fit in at the Bannockburn."

"Shall we take you home?"

"I'll catch the bus near the hotel."

"I don't mind dropping you off."

"I'll catch the bus," Georgie said.

It had begun to rain when they reached Edinburgh. Although Jack thought about renewing his offer to Georgie, he drove directly to the hotel. "Do you have an umbrella?" he asked.

"Not with me."

"I'll get one from the concierge," he said.

Georgie came into the lobby with him and Anne. The two women stood by the entrance while Jack arranged for an umbrella. "For what it's worth, I agree with you completely. I don't think Jack should go anywhere near McPherson," Georgie said.

"My problem is that he's stubborn. When he gets an idea into his head, it tends to stick."

Jack's return ended their conversation. After a round of hugs, Georgie turned to leave, only to be stopped by Jack. "Do you think Liz would like to join us tonight? She'd be very welcome."

"I don't know what she has on, but I'll ask her."

After Georgie's departure, Jack and Anne headed up to their suite. Anne waited until they were through the door before saying, "You need to be more sensitive with Georgie. She probably didn't want you to drive her home because she's embarrassed about where she's living."

"I didn't think about that."

"No, I know you didn't."

Jack looked at the desk and saw that the telephone light was blinking. "We have a message," he said.

"Who knows to contact us here?"

"Harry. Or one of the kids could have spoken to Pam," he said. He picked up the phone, followed the prompts, and listened. "The call was from Ross Goldsmith, vice-chairman of the Pilgrim board."

"What does he want?"

"He wants me to contact him right away. He sounded like it's urgent."

Anne sighed. "Go ahead and call him back."

"Are you sure?"

"Jack, I know if you don't, you won't be able to focus on the dinner tonight. Just do me a favour and try to keep it short."

"Okay."

"I'm going to lie down. If I fall asleep, wake me around six so I have time to get ready for dinner."

Jack waited until Anne had gone into the bedroom and closed the door before reaching for the phone. He hadn't been exaggerating when he told Anne there was urgency in Goldsmith's message, which had been simply "Call me. We need to talk." *Has my proposal been shot down already?* he thought as he dialled Boston.

"Mr. Goldsmith, please. This is Jack Anderson calling."

"One moment, Mr. Anderson. I'll put you through to his office."

"Mr. Anderson, could you hold on, please," Goldsmith's secretary said a few seconds later. "Mr. Goldsmith is in a meeting, but he asked me to get him when you called."

"I'll wait," Jack said, the certainty growing that he wouldn't like what he was about to hear.

"Jack, how's Scotland?" Goldsmith said when he came on the line.

"The same as it was yesterday."

"Not exactly the same," Goldsmith said, and then paused. "For one thing, I believe you can stop worrying about Pilgrim falling into less experienced hands."

"What are you saying?" Jack asked, rising to his feet.

"As promised, I made some phone calls this morning to feel out the board about the company's succession plans. The response was a bit surprising, but not unwarranted," he said. "When I mentioned the idea of your staying on for another few years, there was an outpouring of support. In fact—and this is not hyperbole—as long you keep generating the numbers you are now, I think your tenure could last as long as you want."

"Even Don Arnold agreed?"

"I won't lie to you, Don was a hard sell. He was resistant at first, but when I told him the majority of the board is onside, he said he would go along with it."

"You are a persuasive man, Ross."

"Truthfully, not much persuading was needed. Your impending departure was a ticking bomb that no one wanted to be first to acknowledge. When I pointed out that your departure didn't need to happen, nearly everyone voiced their support for your staying."

"How about the Young resolution?"

"We'll deal with that at the next board meeting."

"And who will tell Gordon?"

"Don will take him out to dinner the night before the meeting and advise him that we've asked you to stay on," Goldsmith said. "Who knows, it might come as a relief to him. Filling your shoes was never going to be an easy task, and not all number-two men are qualified to be a number one."

"This is wonderful news. I'd hoped for it but I can't say I expected it. Thank you, Ross. Thank you so very much."

"There's nothing to thank me for, Jack. Your record speaks for itself."

"And thank you for getting back to me so quickly. I didn't expect that either."

"I've known you a long time, Jack. I know how you worry about things. I could imagine you spending the rest of your holiday fretting about how the board would react, and after the responses I got, there was no sense in waiting. So now you should be able to relax and enjoy the rest of your holiday."

"Believe me, that's what I'm going to do."

"We'll talk when you get home," Goldsmith said.

Jack put the phone back in its cradle and sat down on the desk chair. "Yes, yes, yes!" he said, a huge grin splitting his face. He tried to think of the last time he had felt such joy. When he was first named Pilgrim's president? When Allison was born? But as happy as those events had been, they hadn't given him such a rush. Goldsmith's phone call had validated his career at Pilgrim and every sacrifice he'd made. A future filled with empty days had been put off, as Goldsmith had indicated, indefinitely. What a wonderful word that was, he thought.

Jack heard a noise from the bedroom and realized Anne was still awake. She was sure to ask him about the phone call. What should he tell her? How would she react if he told her the truth? She could be happy for him or exactly the opposite. Better to wait, he decided, until they were back in Boston and everything was official.

The bedroom door opened and Anne came back into the living area. "I don't think I'm going to be able to nap," she said.

"We're going to dinner soon enough anyway."

"Did you reach Ross?"

"I did."

"What did he want?"

"He'd just seen a preview of the last quarter's results

and was thrilled with them. He called me to pass along his congratulations."

"That's wonderful, Jack. You're certainly leaving with a bang, but anyone who knows you wouldn't expect it to be any other way."

19

WHEN JACK STEPPED THROUGH the front doors of the Bannockburn, he immediately thought of the Locke-Ober restaurant in Boston. Locke-Ober was more than a hundred years old, and its mahogany panelling, ornate French furniture, sculptures, oil paintings, silver cutlery, English china, starched white tablecloths, and traditional, beef-heavy menu had made it a favourite among Boston bankers, who could walk there from the nearby financial district. The Bannockburn's furniture was somewhat plainer, but otherwise it compared favourably.

It was ten minutes to seven. As the hosts, Jack and Anne had arrived early. There were going to be six of them for dinner; Georgie had called at six-fifteen to say Liz would be joining them.

The maître d' welcomed them at the door.

"We'll be six, not five," Jack said. "I assume that's fine."

"Not a problem, sir," the maître d' said.

Their table was against a wall near the middle of the restaurant. They had no sooner sat down when Georgie and a tall, auburn-haired young woman appeared at the door. Anne and Jack stood to meet them, and Anne noticed that Georgie was smiling broadly. When they reached the table, Anne held out her hands. "You must be Liz. It's so nice to meet you. You are a gorgeous young woman."

"Why, thank you," Liz said, blushing.

Anne turned to Jack. "Doesn't she look like Allison? The same auburn hair, and those beautiful blue eyes."

"I'm Jack, by the way, and she's Anne," he said to Liz. "Forgive my wife's enthusiasm. She's excited to meet you."

"The same goes for me. You're all I've heard about for the past two days."

"Allison is Jack and Anne's daughter," Georgie said to Liz. "As I remember, she's the oldest of their children and lives in Los Angeles with someone who's in the film industry."

"That's absolutely correct," Anne said.

"There are Harry and Barbara," Jack said suddenly. "Everyone is so punctual."

"It must be a family trait," Anne said.

After a round of greetings, everyone settled into their chairs and a waiter arrived with the drinks menu. "Now, this dinner is on me, and I want you to have whatever you want to drink," Jack said.

"Actually, I want us to share a bottle of Champagne to start, but I want to pay for it," Georgie said. "This is an evening to celebrate. Liz had some very good news today."

"Mum!" Liz said. "You promised you wouldn't."

"I said I'd think about it. I did, and now I want everyone to know. We haven't had much to celebrate lately, but then Jack and Anne show up on our doorstep, and the day after, you hear from Pitlochry. I think fate has decided to be kind to us. It would be inviting bad luck not to acknowledge it," Georgie said.

"Pitlochry? The festival?" Barbara said to Liz.

"Aye, Aunt Barbara, the festival."

"That's so wonderful!"

"Tell us what happened," Harry said.

"Liz has been offered a position in the coming season's ensemble cast," Georgie said.

"You'll be there for the entire season?" Harry asked.

"I will."

"I'm so happy for you," he said.

"Pardon my ignorance, but what is the Pitlochry Festival?" Anne asked.

"Pitlochry is a charming little town about an hour and a half north of here. It's a major entry point to the Highlands and attracts tourists from all over the world. They built a theatre there, right next to the River Tummel, about thirty years ago. It's a repertory company that rotates four or five shows throughout the summer. Some people claim that in the U.K. only Stratford is more important in terms of festival theatre."

"That's very impressive," Anne said, smiling at Liz. "How many shows will you be in?"

"I think I'll be the ingenue in a couple and a supporting cast member in two more," she said. "I won't know all the details until I meet with the artistic director."

"Will you live in Pitlochry?" Barbara asked.

"Of course she will," Georgie said. "The season runs from May to October, and with rehearsals starting very soon, my girl is going to be gone for more than six months."

"Has all this been finalized?" asked Harry.

"I go to Pitlochry tomorrow to sign my contract."

"You'll take the train?" he asked.

"That's my plan."

"Why don't we drive you?" Anne suggested. "We have no plans for tomorrow, and if Pitlochry is as nice as you say, it will give us a chance to see it and at least part of the Highlands."

"I couldn't ask you to do that," Liz said.

"You didn't ask. We offered," Anne said. "It will also give us a chance to get to know you better."

"I think that's a great idea," Jack said.

"I do too," Georgie said. "And if no one objects, I'll come along. I know Pitlochry and can show you some of the sights."

"I think that settles things," Jack said, raising his arm to attract the attention of the waiter.

"Jack, I insist on paying for the bottle of Champagne," Georgie said.

"That isn't going to happen, and there's no point in arguing with me," he said as the waiter arrived. Jack glanced quickly at the menu. "Two bottles of the Pommery Champagne, please."

When the waiter left, Harry said to Jack, "If you don't mind me saying, you seem especially cheery tonight. Did something happen today in Glasgow?"

Jack turned to Georgie. "Did you tell Harry about our day at the Tartan Rover?"

"I haven't had a chance."

"We found McPherson. We didn't see him, but we were told he's still alive," Jack said to Harry.

"That is a surprise. I was expecting—or maybe I should say hoping—that he was dead. Did you find out where he lives?"

"No, but we learned he's a regular at the pub, and the owner has promised to call me when he shows up."

"You want to meet him?"

"Georgie isn't interested, but I am," Jack said. "I have some questions for him."

"I imagine you do."

"Have you seen the photo of him that Georgie has?"

"I have."

"The family resemblance is unmistakable."

"That may be true, but Georgie and I didn't actually exist when our mother left him. There's nothing about the man that holds the slightest interest for me. He has no connection to my life," said Harry.

"So I can't convince you to come with me to the Tartan Rover?"

"No."

"Then I'll stop talking about it."

"Jack, I don't want you to think I'm being insensitive. I do understand there are things you want to know," Harry said, and then paused. "Look, if you don't want to do it alone, I'll go with you. But I'll do it as your brother and not as McPherson's son. I don't even want to be introduced to him."

"That's extraordinarily considerate of you," Jack said. "I may take you up on that offer."

The waiter arrived with the two bottles of Champagne, which halted that conversation. They watched in silence as he opened the first bottle with a loud pop and then poured six glasses. "Shall I open the second bottle and leave it on ice?" he asked.

"Excellent idea," Jack said.

Anne raised her glass. "Here's to a wonderful summer for Liz, and a brilliant start to a long and successful career."

After they drank, Jack picked up the menu. "We should decide what to have for dinner," he said.

As they were reading the menu and chatting about the options, Jack noticed that Anne kept staring at Liz. He was about to say something when she said, "Liz, I don't mean to be nosy, but tell me, is that your natural hair texture or do you straighten it?"

"I straighten it as much as I can." Liz laughed. "Why do you ask?"

"I told you earlier that you remind me of our Allison, except her hair is curly and can get frizzy."

"So is mine unless I work on it."

"My other children don't look anything like her; they all resemble Jack. I always thought there had to be someone in my background with curly auburn hair, but when I look at you . . ."

"Mum was long and lean, exactly like Liz. She also had dark blue eyes, and I have some old colour snaps of her that show a wild mop of auburn hair," Georgie said. "She was a real beauty."

Anne glanced at Jack and then turned back to Georgie. "I think I'd like to see some of those photos, and Allison might too."

"I'll bring them with me tomorrow. You can have a look at them and let me know if you'd like copies."

"That would be lovely."

"Let's order," Jack interrupted. "I'm hungry enough to eat a horse."

"It that's your way of trying to change the subject, I do wish you would be more subtle," Anne said.

He started to protest but then smiled. "I apologize. All I've had to eat today was a Scotch pie. Any subtlety I might have has been overtaken by hunger."

20

THEY ARRIVED IN PITLOCHRY at five to eleven the next morning, after a ninety-minute drive from Edinburgh. It was slightly overcast when Jack pulled into the parking lot of the Festival Theatre, but the sky seemed to be clearing. The clean, crisp air felt like the prelude to a beautiful day.

It had been past ten when they finished dinner the night before. After the Champagne, two bottles of red wine, and after-dinner drinks, no one was feeling any pain. The conversation hadn't returned to either Jessie or Douglas McPherson, instead focusing on lighter topics, such as the plays Liz was going to be in that summer.

Anne had expected Jack to say something about Georgie and their mother's photos as they walked back to the hotel, but he hadn't raised the subject and instead talked about the possibility of inviting their new Scottish family to visit them in the United States. The idea had caught Anne so off guard that she stopped walking and looked up at her husband to see if he was serious. "What's happened to you?" she asked. "You've been in such a good mood this evening."

"I really like Harry and Georgina, and Liz is a sweetheart. If Harry and Barbara's kids are anything like her, they'll fit in with our gang very well."

"Let's get to the end of the week before we start thinking about issuing invitations," she said.

They had gone to bed as soon as they reached their room, and within a few minutes they were asleep. Jack had wakened at six and spent two hours answering Pam's faxes. He had been rigorous in the previous days, but somehow his work this morning took on an extra edge. He wondered how Pam and the rest of his support team were going to react to the news that he was staying on as CEO. They had expressed what he had thought was genuine, deeply felt regret when he announced his decision to retire. Would they be pleased to learn he wasn't going anywhere? He thought they would, but he had learned you could never take for granted how staff really felt about a boss until he was out the door and it was safe to express a true opinion.

Jack ordered coffee and toast at seven and woke Anne when it arrived. At five to nine they made their way downstairs to find Georgie and Liz waiting for them in the lobby.

"Another day, another adventure," Anne said as the women exchanged hugs.

"Good morning, ladies. I ordered the car for nine, so I think it should be here," Jack said.

"Do you need help with directions?" Georgie asked.

"No, I went over the map with the concierge. It seems to be a pretty straight run."

"Good. Then I can nap."

There wasn't much conversation during the car ride. Georgie slept, Liz read a script, and Anne took in the scenery.

They got out of the car in the Festival Theatre's parking lot. "How much time do you need?" Georgie asked Liz.

"Signing the contract won't take long, but I don't know how involved things will be with the artistic director. It could be several hours. What do you plan to do?"

Georgie checked her watch. "I thought we'd take a walk through the town and then visit Blair Castle. We could check back here after that. If you're not done, we'll take a tour at the Edradour Distillery. And I thought it would be nice to end the day with tea at the Green Park Hotel."

"Why don't I meet you at the Green Park around three? I can't imagine I'll be much later than that. If I'm early, I'll sit in the bar and look out at Loch Faskally."

"That's it then, we're set," Georgie said, and held out her arms for a hug. "Good luck, my love. I'm sure it will all go very well."

Liz smiled at them all. "Have a great visit. We used to come here all the time. It's one of my favourite places in Scotland."

"How far is it from here to the town?" Jack asked.

"About a mile. It's an easy walk. See that small collection of houses down there by the river? The area is called Port-na-Craig, and there's a wee footbridge that leads directly into town," Georgie said. "But if you want to see Blair Castle, we'll have to drive. It's in Blair Atholl, about seven miles away."

"Blair Atholl? Moira mentioned that name when she told us your husband's," said Jack.

"It's a village, and there is a connection — in a way that only the Scots can conjure up," she said. "Atholl's mother's family name was Murray. Blair Castle has been the ancestral home of the Murray clan for more than seven hundred years, and the head of the clan carries the title Duke of Atholl."

"Despite — or maybe because of — the connection, I'm not sure I'm up for another castle tour," Jack said. "The distillery interests me, though."

"After all that we drank last night, how can you even think about alcohol?" Anne asked.

"It's actually far more interesting than you would think," Georgie said. "The distillery is a hundred and fifty years old and is the smallest in Scotland."

"How small is that?"

"Three employees. It's owned by a French liquor conglomerate now, but they haven't changed the way it operates."

"How can they turn a profit with an operation that small?" Jack asked.

"They specialize. As I recall, they have a ten-year-old single malt that's expensive and always in demand."

"Sounds good to me," Jack said.

Georgie looked at Anne, who was frowning. "We can walk to the distillery from here. It's about three miles, with a lot uphill. It's a beautiful day for a walk, and when we're finished there, we can walk back through town to the Green Park Hotel. There are a few stores along the way that sell Scottish goods you might find interesting."

"I like the idea of a good walk," Anne said.

"Then let's do it," Jack said.

It took close to an hour to get to Edradour, and by the time they reached the white-painted wrought-iron fence that enclosed it, Anne had worked up a sweat. They stood at the entrance, looking up the driveway at a whitewashed brick building surrounded by cottages, all with red doors. Georgie pushed open the gate and walked towards the main building.

"Can I help you?" a man asked, appearing out of nowhere.

"We're here for a tour," Georgie said.

"Sorry, but you're a few weeks too early. The season hasn't started yet."

"That's too bad. I was boasting about your single malt to my brother and his wife, who are here from the United States. He's rather rich and famous, and he loves whisky," Georgie said. "Besides, we've walked all the way from Port-na-Craig."

The man smiled and said, "How can I possibly say no when you put it like that?"

An hour later they began the downhill walk from the distillery to Pitlochry's main street. Jack now knew everything imaginable about distilling and ageing whisky. He was also the new owner of two cases of ten-year-old single malt, which were scheduled to arrive in Wellesley sometime later in the year, after the whisky had been uncasked and bottled.

They took their time getting to town and then made their leisurely way from store to store until they reached the Green Park Hotel. Georgie and Anne shopped as they went. Jack occasionally poked his head into a store but most often stayed outside on the sidewalk, watching people go by. He couldn't remember the last time he had felt so relaxed.

With Anne carrying three shopping bags, they left the commercial part of town and walked past rows of houses separated from the road by a narrow sidewalk. Ahead on their left, Jack spotted the sign for the Green Park.

"This hotel was a country house roughly a hundred years ago," Georgie said. "They've added to it, but the new buildings are completely in tune with the old house."

"It's beautiful," Anne said, admiring the whitewashed brick structures with their grey slate roofs.

"I think it's even nicer at the back. There's a large lawn that sweeps down to Loch Faskally. When I came here in the past, I would sit by the loch for hours on end. It was so peaceful."

As they approached the main building, Liz came out of its front door with a bundle of manila folders tucked under her arm.

"Have you been here long?" Georgie asked.

"About fifteen minutes. I got a ride from the assistant director, who has rented a house halfway between here and Blair Atholl. She has a spare room, which she offered to me."

"How lucky is that!" Georgie said.

"It's very lucky. Besides not having to find a place to live, I'll have professional advice close at hand whenever I need it."

"And how was your meeting with the artistic director?" Anne asked.

"Just wonderful. He couldn't have been kinder. He gave me this armful of scripts with my lines clearly marked and told me how much he was looking forward to working with me."

"How many plays are you in?"

"Four."

"Will it be difficult learning your lines for that many?"

"Well, I'm not the lead in any of them, so I don't have much to learn. But in addition to those I'm the understudy for the lead role in *Little Shop of Horrors*, so that will be a bit more work. Rehearsals begin in early April and I want to be fully prepared. Mum is going to be tired of listening to me."

"No, I will not," Georgie said. "I'm so proud of you that you can recite your lines day and night for all I care."

"We're all proud of you," Anne said.

"Yes, well done," Jack added.

"We'll have a drink to celebrate," Georgie said.

"Not here we won't," Liz said. "The bar is closed, and lunch ended at two."

"That's my fault. I had forgotten their hours of operation," Georgie said. "Oh well, we'll walk back to town. There are a couple of places on the way."

"That reminds me, I should give Harry a call. We haven't organized anything for tonight," said Jack.

"You aren't tired of us yet?" Georgie asked.

"Don't be silly."

"I was joking," Georgie said. "There's a post office in the centre of town with phone boxes. It's across the street from a little restaurant I like."

"Then let's go."

21

AS THEY WERE DRIVING back from Pitlochry after their late lunch, it began to rain heavily. They motored down the M90 towards Edinburgh, but traffic slowed to a crawl as they neared the city. Jack was usually impatient in situations like that, but two Scotches with lunch and the company of three happy women had mellowed him.

The women had talked incessantly throughout the entire journey, Georgie and Anne thrilled by Liz's success and Liz getting caught up in their excitement. Jack smiled as he listened. The trip to Scotland couldn't have been more appropriately timed. It hadn't started well with Moira, but she was now a distant memory that had been completely overshadowed by Harry and Georgie. Of the two, he was most drawn to Georgie. Despite their differences about their mother, he admired her. She had gone through hell, but instead of giving up, she was getting on with her life. So was her daughter, who more and more reminded him of Allison.

"What time are we meeting Harry and Barbara?" Georgie asked from the back seat as they reached the outskirts of Edinburgh.

"Seven."

"Will that give us enough time to freshen up and change?" Anne asked.

"I figure we'll be at the hotel by six-fifteen, and Harry says the Italian restaurant he recommended is a ten-minute cab ride."

"We're not going home, so don't worry about us," Georgie said. "We'll wait for you in the hotel lobby."

"Nonsense. You can come up to our suite," Anne said. "And you can use our bathroom if you need one."

Twenty minutes later, Jack dropped off the car at the hotel entrance and they all made their way upstairs. Liz, Georgie, and Jack sat in the living room while Anne changed. When she came back, he headed for the bathroom, where he brushed his teeth, washed his face, and quickly changed shirts. On his return to the living room, he found Anne and Georgie sitting side by side on the couch looking down at Georgie's lap. Georgie glanced up at him with a look that seemed slightly guilty.

"What's going on?" he asked.

"Georgie brought some photos of your mother," Anne said. "She didn't think you would want to see them, so we were taking advantage of your absence."

The photos on Georgie's lap formed a small stack. He

stared at them for a few seconds and then asked, "Does Allison look like her?"

"Both she and Liz do," Anne said. "But why don't you look at them yourself and draw your own conclusions."

Jack hesitated, surprised by how nervous Anne's suggestion made him feel.

"If she is the devil in your life, don't you think it might help to put a face on her?" said Anne.

Georgie patted the couch. "Come and sit next to me. There aren't many to look at, so it won't take long."

Jack stared again at the pile of photos, then crossed over to the couch. He sat down next to Georgie.

"I have them arranged by year," Georgie said. "I'm sure Anne won't mind if I start over."

"Please do," Anne said.

Georgie shuffled the photos and then picked up the oldest. She held it in front of her so everyone could see it. A young girl sat against a plain sheet backdrop and looked into the camera with a hint of a smile. It was a black-and-white photo, but it wasn't hard for Jack to imagine the colour of the wild, curly hair that circled her head like a halo.

"She was fourteen when this was taken. Wasn't she a pretty girl, with those big eyes, that fine nose and delicate mouth?" Georgie said. "I have a school picture of Liz that reminds me of this one. They have the same bone structure, and of course that hair."

"Like Allison," Anne said.

"This one was taken in 1925 by a commercial photographer at a fairground," Georgie said, turning over the photo so Jack could see the handwriting on the back. "She made a note of the year and place."

"If the birthdate on her tombstone is accurate, she was sixteen then," Anne said. "She was likely pregnant with Moira."

"She was just about to turn seventeen when Moira was born," said Georgie.

"Just a girl," Anne said. "I can't imagine being pregnant at that age. I was in my twenties and out of university and still felt overwhelmed by it."

"Me too, and I was almost thirty when Liz was born," Georgie said, and then turned to the next photo.

It was a full-length shot of Jessie standing arm in arm with another woman in front of a shop window. They wore unbuttoned woollen coats over dresses. Jessie's was snug and showed off a slender frame and legs. She had a big grin on her face, as if the women had just shared a joke. The photo was in faded colour, but her hair was undeniably auburn.

"This was taken in 1927," Georgie said, again showing Jack the writing on the back. "With Alice McDonald at Duncan Newsagents. She was Mum's best friend. She died ten years before Mum."

"I was born in 1928," Jack said.

"I know," Georgie said, and then quickly leafed through several pictures before stopping at one. "This is you when you were three."

Jack stared at a picture of a small boy in shorts and a short coat buttoned to the neck, standing on a sand dune and pointing a stick towards the sea. Behind him, sitting on the dune and also warmly dressed, was Jessie, her hair windblown and dishevelled. Her attention was fixed on the boy, who had a determined look on his face. She was smiling broadly.

"'July 1931, an outing to the Irvine shore with my Bonnie Jack,'" Georgie read from the photo's back.

"Are you sure that's your mother's handwriting?" Anne asked.

"Absolutely."

"Why is 'Bonnie' capitalized?"

"Because that's what she called him. It was never just Jack. It was always Bonnie Jack," Georgie said and smiled. "So you see, Bloody Jack isn't your first nickname."

"I think that's lovely," Anne said.

"I don't," Jack muttered. "And I'm not sure I want to see any more of these."

Georgie's hand slipped into his and she squeezed. "One more, please? Just one more?"

"One," Jack said.

Georgie freed her hand from his and slipped out a photo from near the bottom of the stack. "This was taken in September 1934, at Mason's Commercial Photography Studio in Glasgow," she said. "She must have made a special trip, and it would have cost her more money than she could probably afford. The back reads, 'Me and my Bonnie Jack and beautiful Moira.'"

"I hadn't seen this one," Anne said, trying to keep a check on her emotions as tears began to fall.

"I'm not showing this to be cruel, Jack," Georgie said. "All I wanted was for you to see her face."

He looked quickly at the photo and then turned his head away.

"Let me see it," Anne said, extending her hand. Georgie passed it to her. In the photo, Jessie sat on a low stool with her children seated at her feet. Jack's hands were cupped under his chin and his elbows rested on the knees of his crossed legs. He looked bored. Moira's hands were folded neatly in her lap and she was smiling. "Even in faded black-and-white you can see that Jack's shirt is frayed at the cuffs and collar, and that cotton dress of Moira's looks well worn."

"What do you think of Mum?" Georgie asked.

"I hardly know what to think. She looks like a different person from the other photos," Anne said. "She's so skinny, so haggard. Her eyes are sunken and there's no life in them. You can see the hollows in her cheeks. Her mouth is downturned as if all the joy has been wrung out of her. I've rarely seen anyone look so incredibly sad."

"She was just twenty-five at the time, but she looks fifty-five," Georgie said. "This was two months before she left McPherson."

"Pass it to me," Jack said suddenly.

He took the photo from Anne and walked to the window. With his back turned to them, he held it at waist level and stared down at it.

Anne debated going to him, but then she wondered what she could say or do to make it any easier for him, and decided to stay where she was. Georgie started to rise to her feet, but Anne placed her arm across Georgie's lap and shook her head.

No one spoke for several minutes. Liz, sitting in a chair opposite the couch, raised her eyebrows at Anne and Georgie and mouthed, *This is getting uncomfortable.*

"Lizzie, if you have to go to the bathroom, this might be a good time to do it. We'll be leaving for the restaurant shortly," Georgie said.

"That's a great idea," Liz said.

As Liz stood up, Jack turned towards them. "I'm glad I saw this," he said.

Georgie closed her eyes and pressed her lips together. Anne saw tears start to form. "I can't begin to tell you how—" Georgie began, only to be interrupted by the phone ringing.

Jack picked up the phone as it started its third ring. "This is Jack Anderson," he said. Checking his watch, he added, "I'll be there within the next two hours. Do what you can to make sure he doesn't leave."

"McPherson?" Georgie asked.

"Yes. That was the Tartan Rover. He's there."

"What are you going to do?" Anne asked.

"I'm going to the pub."

"Right now? Didn't Harry say he would go with you?"

"He did."

"Then don't you think it would be appropriate to give him the chance?" Anne said. "I suggest that we go to the restaurant as planned, and then the two of you can leave together from there."

"The barman did say that McPherson generally stays the night. I don't think there's any need to rush," Georgie said.

"What time does the pub close?" he asked.

"Eleven, with last orders at ten-thirty."

He looked at his watch again. "Okay, we'll go to the restaurant. But don't expect me to eat."

"Jack, are you sure this is the right thing to do?" Georgie asked.

"There's no point in talking to him about this anymore," Anne said. "When he's this determined, nothing can change his mind."

"Then I'll stay quiet," Georgie said.

"One thing, though," Jack said. "Can I keep this photo?"

"Of course. I have another copy," she said. "And here, take the one of you and Mum on the dune."

"Thank you," he said as he slipped the pictures into his blazer pocket.

22

SALVATORE'S WAS A BOISTEROUS, unpretentious place imbued with a wonderful aroma of garlic. It was exactly the type of Italian restaurant Jack enjoyed — except he wasn't staying.

Harry stood up to greet them as they approached. "How was your day in Pitlochry?" he asked.

"It was fine. I'll tell you about it on the way to Glasgow," Jack said.

"Glasgow?"

"The guy at the Tartan Rover pub just called. McPherson is there now."

"So you're intent on going through with this?"

"Jack is determined, and I've been told there's no use in arguing with him," Georgie said.

"Do we at least have time for dinner?" Harry asked.

"I don't want to risk missing him," Jack said.

"Then I guess we're off to Glasgow," Harry said with a quick glance at Barbara. "Am I driving?"

"If you would, I'd appreciate it," Jack said.

"I've told Harry I'm not happy with this idea of meeting McPherson," Barbara said to Jack.

"He doesn't have to come," Jack said to her.

"Yes, I do. I'm not going to let you do this by yourself," said Harry. "God knows what could happen to an American wandering around that part of Glasgow alone at night."

"If that's what you're worried about, Harry, I think I'd better come with you. I'm the only one here who actually knows her way around Glasgow and how to handle Glaswegians," Georgie said.

"I thought McPherson scared you," Jack said.

"He does. I'm expecting you and Harry to keep me safe."

"We will," Jack said.

"Mum, do you want me to come with you?" Liz asked.

"No, this is something my brothers and I have to deal with by ourselves."

"Then let's go," Jack said, and turned to Anne. "We'll meet you back at the hotel. I can't imagine we'll be late."

"Yes, please don't be late. And if there's any kind of a problem, call me at the hotel."

"Worry not," Jack said, bending down to kiss his wife.

Harry's Jaguar was parked nearby. They piled in, with

Georgie, again acting as navigator, sitting in the front with Harry.

They were quiet for the first part of the trip, each absorbed in their own thoughts. Harry broke the silence as they neared Glasgow. "How old is McPherson?"

"Eighty-two. He was fifty-five when he was sent to prison for manslaughter, and almost seventy by the time he got out."

"And he's had a clean record since then?" Harry said.

"As far as I know, but I didn't spend much time researching his life after prison."

"What made you look for him in the first place?" Harry asked.

"Mum's horror stories about him got to me, and despite everything he did to her, I always thought that deep down she wanted to know what had happened to him."

"She didn't still care for him, did she?" Harry asked in disbelief.

"Of course not. But like it or not, he had been a big part of her life. I guess as she was getting close to death she wanted some kind of closure where he was concerned."

"But she had been dead for quite some time before you found out where he was," Jack said.

"That's true."

"So why did you keep looking?"

"Why did you come to Scotland?"

"To see Moira."

"That's only part of it, Jack. Another reason — and

maybe the biggest, from everything you've said — is that you wanted to know why our mother abandoned you," Georgie said. "You came here searching for answers about her."

"But why did *you* keep looking for him?"

"He's my father," she said.

"Come on, Georgie!" Harry blurted.

"Harry, like it or not, he is our biological father. I know that seems abstract, but the more I thought about it, the less abstract it got. I mean, his impact on Mum was profound. He shaped the woman that she became, and the way she raised us was at least partially a reflection of the way he treated her. So even if it was in a second-hand way, he had a bearing on our lives."

"Like Jessie had on mine," Jack said. "Thanks to her, I'm mistrustful of just about everyone I meet, and that makes me cold and calculating. That, I think, is Jessie's legacy for me. Any humanity I have comes from my late adoptive parents, Anne, and my kids."

"That last bit sounds like an exaggeration," Georgie said.

"No, it's the truth. I've always felt like I'm alone on an island, and the only way to survive is to keep everyone else off it," he said, and then smiled. "I didn't get the nickname Bloody Jack by being a nice guy. I trust no one. Everyone is disposable."

"That's in business, but what about with your family, with Anne?" asked Georgie.

"I love Anne, but there are things I don't tell her, and

some of those things she has a right to know. What does that say about me?"

"You have trust issues. But then, why wouldn't you?" Harry said.

"Exactly. Why wouldn't I?"

Georgie looked out the window. "We're almost at the pub," she said. "I just felt a chill on the back of my neck saying that."

A few minutes later the car stopped in front of the dimly lit Tartan Rover. To Jack's eyes it looked even grungier than it had the day before.

They got out of the car and stood together awkwardly on the sidewalk before Jack finally said, "What the hell," and headed for the door. He stepped inside and was immediately engulfed in cigarette smoke and noise. The pub was packed. A quick glance located no empty tables.

"Can I help you?" the barman said.

Jack walked over to him, with Harry and Georgie alongside. "We're back. Is our man still here?" he asked.

"He is. Where's my forty pounds?"

Jack took the money from his wallet and laid it on the bar. "Where is he?"

"Over there in the far corner to your right. He's with his mate Duff."

"Thank you," Jack said, turning to look in that direction.

"Before you bother the wee man, you should know that I told him some people were asking for him," the barman said. "I thought it was the right thing to do. I didn't want to risk you scaring Dougie to death."

"That isn't likely," Jack said. "How did he react when you told him?"

"He couldn't have cared less."

"Well, you heard the man. He's here," Jack said to Harry and Georgie. "Do you want me to make the approach alone or shall we do it together?"

"Together," Georgie said without hesitation.

"I agree," added Harry, "but what should we say to him?"

"As simple as it sounds, I thought I'd start with hello and see where that leads," Jack said.

"Let's do it," said Harry.

The corner the barman had indicated wasn't as well lit as the rest of the room, and the two men sitting at the table were in partial darkness. It wasn't until he was about ten feet from them that Jack saw McPherson clearly. He was engaged in an animated conversation with a younger, larger man sitting next to him. Unsurprisingly, McPherson looked like an older version of the man in Georgie's photo. His hair was white but still thick, and combed straight back; it looked greasy. His face was laced with deep lines, and the sides of his mouth sagged around a prominent chin. A furrowed brow sat above eyes that were small and black. As McPherson spoke, Jack saw he was missing several bottom teeth and an incisor. He was dressed in a baggy grey wool suit that had black stains on the lapels and around the cuffs. His white shirt had been stained at the collar by something yellow.

The man sitting next to him looked to be about Jack's age. He wore blue jeans and a denim shirt that was stretched across a large belly. He was completely bald and had only traces of eyebrows. When he laughed at something McPherson said, Jack saw that he also lacked a full set of teeth. The younger man looked to be about twice the size of McPherson, but his attitude towards the older man was one of reverence. *What an odd couple*, Jack thought.

Whatever conversation the two men were having halted momentarily as they reached for the beers that sat on the table. Jack took advantage of the break to approach them. "Excuse me," he said.

McPherson looked up at him. There was an almost comical moustache of beer foam above his mouth, but there wasn't anything funny about the eyes that bore into Jack. "Are you the lot Robbie said was asking about me?" he rasped.

"We are," Jack replied.

"What the fuck do you want?"

"We thought we'd start by introducing ourselves."

"You're interrupting a private chat."

"This won't take long."

"It's taken long enough already. Why don't the lot of you just fuck right off."

"You are Douglas Andrew McPherson, are you not?" Jack said.

"He sounds like a Yank," Duff said, nudging

McPherson. "What does a Yank want with you? It might be worth finding out."

McPherson nodded. "Are you a Yank?" he said to Jack.

"I am."

"Well, for your information, no one calls me Andrew anything. My name is Dougie."

"But you were Andrew, correct? Before you went to prison?"

McPherson's eyes narrowed. "You seem to know a lot about me. What's your name?"

"Jack Anderson."

"And those two eejits standing behind you, do they have names?"

"Harry Montgomery and Georgina Malcolm."

"I've never heard of any of you."

"Actually, you and I have met," Jack said.

"I don't remember you, and my memory's still good."

Before Jack could offer a response, Georgie pushed forward and leaned in close to McPherson. "Do you remember a woman named Jessie McPherson? She was your wife," she said loudly.

McPherson pointed a bony finger at her. "Who do you think you're talking to like that?" he said.

"Why don't you just answer my question."

"Fuck off, the lot of you," McPherson said.

"She was your wife, you bastard!" Georgie said.

"She was a diddy bitch. I was well rid of her," McPherson said, his voice becoming agitated.

"You should leave Dougie alone unless you want me to get involved," Duff said.

"All I want is to introduce myself," Jack said to Duff. "I'm Dougie's son. My name used to be Jack McPherson."

Duff turned to look at McPherson, who was now staring at Jack, his mouth wide open.

"And I'm your daughter," Georgie barked. "My mother, Jessie, was pregnant with me when she ran away from you."

"Dougie, what the hell is going on here?" Duff said.

McPherson glanced at Georgie, but then his eyes returned to Jack. He continued to stare at him, his expression a mixture of curiosity and confusion.

"Did you hear what I said about my mother, about Jessie?" Georgie persisted.

McPherson waved a hand in her direction as if swatting away a fly. "Even if she was pregnant, you're not mine. She was a whore, that woman. Why do you think I threw her out?" he said, his composure returning.

"You threw no one out. She escaped from you and took us with her," Georgie said. She looked at Duff. "Beating women was all this man was good for. He's nothing but a coward."

McPherson put his hands on the table and stood up. Jack noticed Duff flinch. Then McPherson hawked, leaned forward and spat. A spray of spittle and phlegm hit Georgie in the face. She reeled back and then swung wildly at McPherson. As her fist went by him, he threw a punch that connected with her mouth. She crumpled to the ground.

McPherson looked down at her with a satisfied smile on his face.

Jack yelled as he drove a fist into McPherson's nose. He heard a crack and saw blood fly in all directions. McPherson fell back, but before he hit the ground Jack punched him again. Then it was Duff's turn. His fist hit Jack a glancing blow on the side of the head. Jack lashed out with his arm, trying to fend him off. Duff took a step back, broke his pint glass over the edge of the table, and waved its jagged edges at Jack.

"Enough!" someone shouted.

Duff froze. Jack turned to see the barman standing with a cricket bat in his hand.

"These fuckers started this!" Duff said, and then looked down at the floor. "The Yank tried to kill Dougie, and I think he might have done it."

23

THE UNCONSCIOUS MCPHERSON WAS taken to hospital in an ambulance. Duff kept asking the attendants if they thought McPherson was going to die. They refused to offer any opinion, but Jack thought he detected signs of concern in their manner.

They treated Georgie in the pub. She had a split upper lip and one of her front teeth was loose. They advised her to keep the lip well iced. Duff's punch to Jack's head hadn't done any visible damage.

A police constable arrived ten minutes after the fracas. After hearing various versions of what had happened, he told Jack, Georgie, Harry, and Duff that they couldn't leave the pub. Thirty minutes later, an inspector arrived with a sergeant and two more constables. The police first spoke to witnesses who had been sitting at nearby tables. Then Harry was interviewed.

When they had finished with him, Harry came over to talk to Jack. "They're letting me go," he said.

"I'm not sure that will be the case for me," Jack said. "Will you go to the hotel and let Anne know what's happening?"

"That was my intention."

"Then find me a very good lawyer. I don't know if they're going to hold Georgie as well, but you should retain him for both of us, just in case."

"I'm on my way," Harry said.

The pub was now vacant except for the police, Duff, Georgie, Jack, and Robbie the barman. The police had separated them as best they could and were conducting interviews in one corner. Jack watched as they talked to Duff, who kept pointing to him. As with Harry, they let him leave when they had finished taking his statement.

Georgie was next, and the interview went on substantially longer than the others. She was very emotional and twice was given a paper napkin to wipe her eyes. Finally the police inspector got up and helped Georgie to her feet. One of the constables walked her to the door. Now it was just the police and Jack.

"I am Inspector Johnson," the man said as he sat down next to Jack. "This is a real mess you've caused here."

"I don't believe I should talk to you without my lawyer present," Jack said.

Johnson sighed. He was in his thirties, Jack guessed, but had the weary, resigned look of someone who had already seen too much. "Let's not blow this out of proportion, shall we," he said. "This was a pub fight with—from what I've heard—some extenuating and very complicated circumstances. Right now, all I want is your version of the events. Completely off the record."

Jack looked at him and saw sincerity. "The man I hit was convicted of killing a man with a knife in a pub fight, and then he killed another man while he was in prison."

"We know Dougie isn't a saint."

"My point is, he spat at and then punched my sister in the mouth. I had no idea what else he might try to do to her. I stepped in to defend her."

"His friend Duff claims he was provoked. He says you imposed yourselves on him."

"We hardly imposed. We simply approached him to say hello. He's responsible for everything that ensued."

"Why did you approach him in the first place?"

"We wanted to introduce ourselves. He's our father."

"Do you have an idea how strange that sounds?"

"It's still the truth."

Johnson nodded and sighed again. "Your sister tells me you're a successful businessman in America."

"I am."

"So retaining a good lawyer shouldn't be any hardship for you."

"No. Harry is working on that now."

"Good, because you might need one," Johnson said. "And that ends our off-the-record discussion."

"I see."

"I'm taking you to the station house for a formal interview. We'll tell you your rights when we get there, so I wouldn't say much more right now."

"Am I being charged with a crime?"

"That's not for me to say. My superior will make that decision after the interview," Johnson said. "I also have to add that, depending on what happens with McPherson, any charges may be amended."

"Will I be released after the interview?"

"That's not my decision either."

"What's your best guess?"

"I think you should expect to spend the night with us."

24

HARRY HIRED A LAWYER named Duncan Pike. He was a tall, gaunt man with thinning grey hair that he combed over. But other than the hair, he had a distinguished air about him. Just the mention of his name made an impression on the police officers at the station.

When he had arrived at the station, Jack had refused to be interviewed without a lawyer present. At that point Inspector Johnson and Chief Inspector Henderson, his superior, had a discussion about where he should be held.

"He should be in a cell," Henderson said.

"He's hardly a risk. Why don't we let him sit in the interview room? If we need to, we can always move him."

"Who is your lawyer?" Henderson asked Jack.

"I don't know yet. My brother is engaging one as we speak."

Henderson looked at his watch. "We'll give it a couple of hours, but I can't leave you in the interview room all night. If your lawyer can't get here until the morning, you'll have to spend the rest of the night in a cell."

"You aren't like our regular customers," Johnson said. "Putting you in a cell with any of them would be like throwing you to the wolves. They're a rough bunch."

"Glasgow is a rough place."

"The Gorbals is, anyway. There are more civilized parts to the city."

Johnson took Jack into the interview room, which contained a plain table with four chairs. "The mirror is two-way. You'll be watched. I'll lock the door from the outside, but we can hear you. So if you need anything, just say it aloud until someone comes."

Jack sat down at the table. After a few minutes the realization of where he was and why he was there began to sink in. What kind of mess had he fallen into? How was Anne going to react? What charge could he be facing? Assault? What if McPherson died? *He isn't going to die,* Jack thought. *Two punches can't do that to a man.* "I'd better stop thinking about this," he muttered. "Think about something else."

Two hours later, with Jack's imagination still veering off in all directions, the door opened and Johnson stuck in his head. "Your lawyer will be here in about an hour. Your brother hired Duncan Pike, so he must be paying a pretty penny to get him out at this time of night. He's one of the very best in Glasgow, if not the entire country."

It took longer than an hour, but Pike finally arrived. "I will talk to my client here in the interview room, so

I need you to turn off the microphones immediately," he said to Johnson as they entered.

"I'll do it right away."

"Thank you," Pike said, and then turned to Jack with his hand extended. "You can call me Duncan. I assume I can call you Jack?"

"Of course, and thanks for coming at such a late hour."

"Not a problem. I can't have such a prominent client spending the night in a Glasgow jail cell."

"Has my brother also retained your services for my sister?"

"I spoke to the chief inspector when I first arrived, and it doesn't seem that she'll be needing me."

"Thank goodness."

"You, on the other hand, most decidedly do."

"It's a complicated business."

"It is, but there's no reason why we can't make things work in our favour. Your brother explained in detail what happened, and the police have briefed me separately. Most of the bystanders they interviewed won't want to get involved, so we can rule them out as witnesses. That leaves five potential witnesses, one of whom is in the hospital and non-communicative. His friend gave a damaging statement to the police, but he's a convicted felon and hardly reliable. On the other hand, your brother and sister and you are all upstanding citizens."

"That's encouraging."

"What we have to do now is hope that McPherson

recovers," Pike said. He paused while he made sure Jack had heard him. "If he dies, the situation changes. By that I mean the process changes, although not necessarily the outcome."

"You'll need to explain that to me."

"If McPherson recovers, if he has no more than a broken nose, odds are you won't be charged with anything. The police will write it off as another pub fight in the Gorbals. We're aided in that regard by McPherson's history," Pike said. "However, if McPherson dies, the police may feel compelled to lay charges. It could be assault, but they might stretch it to manslaughter. We will obviously contest any charge, and hopefully so successfully that it won't go to trial."

"The last thing I want is a trial."

"Of course you don't, and we'll do everything we can to avoid one," Pike said. "Now, the police are waiting outside to begin the formal interview. Inspector Johnson told me that you had an off-the-record chat at the pub. I need to know everything you discussed with him. When that's done, we'll invite them in."

Ten minutes later Jack had finished, and then he spent five minutes answering Pike's questions.

"Nothing you've told me is of real concern," Pike said. "They'll ask the same questions that Johnson asked you at the pub. Give the same answers. The only difference is that they'll repeat themselves several times, framing the questions in slightly different ways to see if they can elicit different answers. When they do, I may interrupt them. If I do, please remain quiet until I tell you it's okay to answer."

"I can do that."

"Then let's begin, shall we," Pike said, rising from his chair and going to the door.

The interview started a few minutes later. Johnson set up a tape recorder on the table and then Henderson joined them. Sitting across from Pike and Jack, they eased into their questions with Henderson asking, "Tell us why you came here from America, and what brought you to the Tartan Rover."

Jack had little difficulty with any of the questions, primarily because he answered them as truthfully as he could. Henderson was hostile at first and voiced some skepticism as Jack related the story of his abandonment as a child and the search for family that had brought him to Scotland. But gradually the chief inspector became less aggressive and the session became more like a conversation than an interrogation. Pike interceded twice to ask Henderson to reframe questions he thought were leading, but otherwise he listened without any visible reaction.

After about an hour, Henderson turned to Johnson. "I think I'm done. Is there anything you'd like to ask?"

Just as Johnson started to reply, there was a knock on the door. "Come," Henderson shouted.

The door opened and a constable stood in the entrance. "Sir, I thought you should know. We've just received a call from the hospital with an update on McPherson."

"Yes? How is he?"

"He's dead."

25

AT THE NEWS OF McPherson's death, Jack broke out in a cold sweat. It had been one thing to consider the prospect of McPherson dying, but it was quite another to face the reality of it.

Pike took the news calmly. He said in an almost blasé tone, "That's unfortunate, but given the man's nature and history, it's a miracle he lived as long as he did."

"Inspector Johnson and I need to talk about this outside," Henderson said.

"We're not going anywhere. Take all the time you need," Pike said.

"They'll be trying to decide what to do with you," Pike said when the policemen had left. "They won't make a decision about charges right now, but they have to decide whether to let you leave with me tonight."

"What do you think they'll do?"

"I expect them to let you go, but with a warning that

you aren't to leave the country. They might ask for your passport."

"That's not a problem for me."

"I'll resist that kind of request anyway."

The policemen were gone about ten minutes and returned with grim looks on their faces. "McPherson is dead all right," Henderson said. "The preliminary report is that he died of a heart attack."

"So it wasn't the direct result of a punch," said Pike.

"The excitement of the fight could have triggered it."

"So could a lifetime of heavy drinking and smoking," said Pike.

Henderson stared at Jack. "We're going to let you leave, but we want you to stay in Scotland until we make a decision about how to proceed."

"How long will that take?" Pike asked.

"We'll have the medical report tomorrow and we won't sit on it, so maybe two days."

"I wasn't planning to leave that soon anyway," Jack said.

"You said you're staying in Edinburgh?" Henderson asked.

"I am, at the North British Hotel."

"Don't change your address without informing us."

"I'll keep you posted if there are changes on our side. I would prefer it if you direct your communications to Mr. Anderson through me," Pike said.

"Of course."

Pike rose slowly to his feet. "Excellent. If there are no

more questions, we will take our leave of you now."

It was raining, and a cold wind snapped at them as they left the station house. Jack shivered. The weather was a perfect reflection of his mood.

"My car is over there," Pike said, pointing to a black Bentley parked under a streetlight.

"The policeman said you live in Glasgow," Jack said.

"That's correct."

"You don't have to drive me to Edinburgh. I'll take a taxi."

"It's been a very long time since I saw a client in the middle of the night. Now that I'm up, I figure I might as well see it through to the end," Pike said. "Besides, I'm charging you a small fortune for all this."

"That's candid of you."

"I didn't think you'd expect anything less than complete honesty."

They got into the Bentley and began the drive through deserted streets. Jack laid his head against the back of a seat that smelled of new leather and closed his eyes. He knew he couldn't sleep, but he wasn't up to further conversation. McPherson was dead, the fact of it hard to accept. In his mind's eye Jack could see the old man clearly, a contorted face with small, dark, beady eyes and a mouth full of spit ready to unload on Georgie. Jack tried to recall how McPherson had looked before they spoke to him, but all he could conjure was a leering, threatening face. *The spit was humiliating enough. Why did he have to punch her as well? If he hadn't done that,* Jack thought, *I wouldn't have reacted the way I did. What choice did he leave me? What kind of man stands by when another man punches a woman?*

He opened his eyes and sat up. They were on the highway, the wet black road stretching empty in front of them.

"Are you feeling all right?" Pike asked.

"I was thinking about what happened in the pub."

"What transpired tonight was not your fault. You were trying to defend your sister, who was being attacked by a man with a violent history."

"I know, but I can't help thinking that we baited McPherson. For certain we caught him off guard with a load of angry emotions."

"If you are charged—and I think assault is the only option they have—that's the case they'll make."

"We had no violent intentions."

"I believe you, but I have to ask, what did you expect from tonight?" Pike said.

"I don't know. I had this need to see him, and I had one question I wanted him to answer."

"Why he refused to take you in when your mother abandoned you?"

"Yes."

"Did you really expect to get a satisfying response?"

"I don't know what I expected."

Pike turned to look at Jack. "I have something to ask you, but before I do, would you be offended if I played the devil's advocate?"

"No."

"Excellent. Well, we can't completely discount the possibility that you may be charged with assault. If so, it could come down to your family's word against Duff's. And despite his seedy past, it isn't inconceivable that a jury would choose to believe him. He would have no reason to lie. A good prosecutor could do a lot with Duff."

"What are you trying to say?"

"I'm trying to find out how far you will go to make sure there are no charges," said Pike.

Jack looked at him. "I suspect you have something in mind."

"I do," he said. "Are you averse to eliminating Duff as a witness?"

"Eliminating him?"

"My choice of words may have been extreme. What I mean is, are you averse to paying him off? He's the only credible witness the police have. If he were to retract the statement he gave to the police, they would have absolutely no basis for laying charges," Pike said. "We need him to say that your sister did not provoke McPherson. And it would be helpful if he said McPherson initiated the violence against you."

"Is that doable?"

"I think it's entirely doable if we pay him enough. Remember, we're dealing with a petty criminal."

"You wouldn't be worried about him going to the police?"

"Not in the least. Besides, precautions would be taken," Pike said. "We wouldn't deal with him directly. We'd work through a third party, the type of men he would be afraid to cross."

"Criminals?"

"I am a criminal lawyer, Jack. There aren't many serious offenders in Glasgow that I don't know on a first-name basis," Pike said. "And just because a man breaks the law and is branded a criminal doesn't make him unreliable. I'd put more trust in some of those villains than I would in most of the lawyers I work with."

Jack looked out the rain-spattered window as he assessed the risk in Pike's suggestion. It didn't take long to decide there wasn't much. "How much money are we talking about?"

"Three thousand pounds should do the trick. I'll put up the money and include it in my fee. You'll never be connected to it."

"Then I think we should do it."

"Excellent. Now don't spend another minute thinking about Duff. The men I'll use to represent us will make it clear to him that if he whispers a word about this to anyone, there will be serious repercussions," Pike said with a tight smile. "Duff will know the men and he'll know the drill. He won't be a problem."

"That's quite a system you have there."

"Well, the way I view it is that all we're doing is saving the courts time, money, and trouble."

"How long will this take?"

"I'll make some phone calls when I get back to Glasgow. By dinnertime tomorrow you should be worry-free."

26

IT WAS ALMOST FIVE a.m. when Jack got back to the hotel. He went up to the suite, and as he put his key in the lock he heard voices inside. He opened the door, and seconds later Anne wrapped her arms around his neck and began to sob. Over her shoulder he saw Georgie standing near the sofa, her swollen lips a mesh of red and purple bruises.

"I was worried sick," Anne said. "Why didn't you call me?"

"I was at the police station."

"Georgie saw them take you away. She came directly here in a taxi. Harry, Barbara, and Liz were with us for a while as well, but they've gone home," Anne said. "You still haven't told me why you didn't call."

"I was too confused when I got to the station, and then after they let me go, all I wanted was to get back to you."

"Harry told us he got you a top-notch lawyer. Did you meet him?"

"His name is Duncan Pike, and he did a hell of a fine job. I owe Harry big thanks for getting him there in the middle of the night."

"You have to call Harry. He's at home, but he's waiting up to hear what happened."

"Nothing terrible will happen. I've been told not to leave Scotland until the police decide if they're going to lay charges, but Pike is confident they won't. We should know something by tomorrow."

"That's wonderful," Georgie said tearfully. "I've been worried sick. I shouldn't have taunted McPherson the way I did. But the moment I saw him, all I could think of was him beating Mum."

Anne grabbed Jack's hand and pulled him into the room. "Georgie's been here with me all night. She's been so supportive. Give her a hug too."

Jack stood there with both women hugging him for what seemed like minutes before gently prying himself free. He took a good look at Georgie's face. "Should you see a doctor about that?"

"I did. The hotel arranged for someone to come up. I'm to keep icing it. There are no broken bones, just a loose tooth."

"That's good news. I was afraid it might be worse than that," he said, and then noticed they were both fully dressed. "Have either of you slept?"

"How could we sleep, given the circumstances?" Anne asked.

"I didn't sleep either. I'm exhausted," he said.

"We'll go to bed in a few minutes, but you have to call Harry first," Anne said.

He sighed. "I could really use a Scotch, but there's no chance of getting one at this hour."

"That's where you're wrong," Anne said. "I ordered a bottle of Scotch and a bottle of gin when I got back from the restaurant. I thought we might need something to tide us over tonight."

"You clever girl."

"Georgie and I have been working on the gin, so there's a full bottle of Scotch for you."

"Pour me a large one, please, while I go to the bathroom," he said.

When Jack came back into the living room, Anne and Georgie were sitting on the sofa. A glass half-filled with Scotch sat on the table in front of them. He picked it up, sipped, and then sipped again. "I'll call Harry now," he said.

Jack sat at the desk and listened to Harry's phone ring five times before he answered.

"Anne?" Harry said.

"It's me, Jack. I'm here at the hotel with Anne and Georgie. I'm going to put you on speakerphone so they can hear you."

"Thank goodness you're back. I wasn't sure what the police were going to do," Harry said. "I guess Pike made it to the station."

"He did, and thanks for hiring him. He's very good, and I needed someone that good. In fact, I still do for at least another day. But if Pike's judgement is correct, we'll be able to put this behind us by the end of tomorrow."

"So no charges?"

"Not yet, and Pike doesn't think any will be forthcoming."

"When I told him what had happened, he thought they might charge you with assault."

"Assault was a lesser concern," Jack said. "About two hours ago we were more worried about a manslaughter charge."

He saw Anne's eyes widen and Georgie's face fall as she reached for Anne's hand.

"What do you mean?" Harry said with a slight stammer.

"McPherson is dead," Jack said, looking at the women and speaking as distinctly as he could.

"Oh no," Anne gasped.

"Awww," Georgie said, closing her eyes.

"All you did was punch him on the nose," Harry said.

"I punched him twice, and he was eighty years old," Jack said. "The good news — if there can be such a thing under these circumstances — is that he died of a heart attack. That raises the question of what caused the heart attack, but Pike doesn't seem fazed by that."

"What is he fazed by?" Harry asked.

"Nothing. He believes things are under control."

"Duff made all kinds of wild accusations. Are the police going to ignore him?"

"Pike believes Duff will retract a lot of what he said," Jack replied. "In fact, he believes he can persuade him to say that McPherson's attack on Georgie was unprovoked and that my actions were in response to McPherson's aggression."

"How will he convince him to do that?"

"Nothing dramatic, but it might be better if you don't know the details," Jack said.

Harry fell silent.

"He died of a heart attack," Jack repeated. "Nothing else matters."

"I wish I'd never heard the name McPherson. I wish I'd left him in the past," Georgie moaned. "What a mess I've caused."

"You can't blame yourself for what happened," Jack said. "If I hadn't come along he would have remained in your past. I was the one who wanted to see him. I should never have involved you and Harry."

"You can't blame yourself either. Who knew the man would react like that?" Harry said. "What's done is done. None of us are at fault. At the end of the day, McPherson was true to his character. He was a sadistic animal — the way he treated Georgie is proof."

"I agree with Harry," Anne said. "There's no value in rehashing what happened. If the lawyer says he has things under control, then I think we should leave things in his hands and get on with our lives."

"Speaking of which, I need to get some sleep. I can't remember the last time I was up this late," Harry said.

"We all need sleep," Jack said. "Does anyone have any plans for tomorrow . . . I mean, today?"

"I'm going to take the day off work," Harry said.

"And I can't work with my face looking like this," said Georgie.

"Then why don't we meet for dinner," Jack said. "By then I might have heard from Pike."

"That sounds like a fine plan," Harry said, and then paused. "I'll say goodnight to you all, then. It was quite a night, but we've come through it in one piece. We've come through it as a family should."

"Amen to that," Anne said.

Jack turned off the speakerphone as Harry hung up, then turned to the women. "I don't mind sleeping on the couch. You two can share the bed."

"No," Georgie said, getting to her feet. "I'm going home. Liz will be worried, and I think I need my own bed."

"But we'll see you tomorrow?" Anne said.

"Of course. I'll let you know as soon as I'm up and functioning."

"Let me wait with you until the taxi comes," Jack said.

"There's no need. Besides, you look absolutely knackered. Get to bed."

They walked Georgie to the door, shared hugs, and watched until she got into the elevator.

"Bed," Anne said to Jack as the elevator doors closed.

As soon as they reached the bedroom, they threw on pajamas and climbed into bed. Jack lay flat on his back.

Anne rested her head on his chest and wrapped an arm around his waist.

"Who could have imagined?" he muttered.

"Tonight was like a bad dream, but as Harry said, we came through it like a family should."

"Maybe we did, but I can't stop thinking that I killed the man who was, for better or worse, the patriarch of that family."

27

THE ROOM WAS DARK when Jack woke, and he wondered if he'd slept at all. Then he saw a sliver of daylight at the bottom of the heavy, tightly drawn curtains. He slid from the bed and opened the door. Anne sat on the sofa reading a newspaper.

"What's the time?" he asked.

"It's past one."

"Is that coffee?" he asked, pointing to a pot on the table in front of her.

"There could be a cup left. You should order more."

He kissed his wife on the forehead, then poured what was left in the pot into a cup, took a sip, and grimaced. "It's cold," he said, and picked up the phone. "Do you want anything besides coffee?"

"No. I don't have much of an appetite."

He called room service, ordered a large pot of coffee, and then sat next to Anne. "How did you sleep?"

"Okay, although one thing kept worrying me. How is Duncan Pike going to persuade that man Duff to come up with a story that helps us? You may not want to tell Harry and Georgie, but I'd like to know."

"He's going to pay him."

"I thought as much — though I did imagine a few more sinister options," she said. "Why didn't you want to tell Georgie and Harry?"

"They live here. I thought it better that they don't know, in case something goes wrong and there's blowback," he said.

"Is Pike confident Duff will co-operate?"

"He is, mainly because of the people he'll use to negotiate with him."

"That does sound more sinister."

"Pike knows the system. We'd be foolish not to let him do his thing."

"You're putting a lot of faith in a man you just met."

"Harry said he comes highly recommended. That was confirmed when I saw how the police treated him," Jack said. "Besides, I like to think I'm a good judge of character, and I felt comfortable with him from the start."

Anne sighed. "Okay, I feel better about Pike, but I am worried about Georgie. She looked frightful last night, and when she called here about half an hour ago, she sounded despondent."

"She went through a lot yesterday. For someone who wasn't sure she even wanted to see McPherson, she certainly let loose the first chance she got."

"It had probably been building up in her for years. I'm not surprised that she couldn't contain her emotions," Anne said.

"What did she say when she called?"

"She and Harry are suggesting a place for dinner tonight that is about three blocks from here."

"That's fine with me."

"Then call Harry and let him know," she said. "I've been waiting for you to get up so I can shower."

Shortly after Anne left for the bathroom, there was a knock at the door from room service. Jack exchanged the old coffee for the new and sat down at the desk with a fresh cup. He phoned Harry. "Hey, it's Jack. How are you feeling?"

"I have mixed emotions. Mainly I regret not trying harder to talk you out of going to the pub."

"Don't beat yourself up about that. I wouldn't have changed my mind," Jack said. "Anne told me that Georgie sounded a bit down when she spoke to her this morning. How did she seem to you?"

"She blames herself for what happened to McPherson."

"The man had a heart attack. It could have happened anywhere, anytime, and for any reason."

"She doesn't care about him; she's concerned that his death will cause you problems. She's a natural worrier, and she won't stop stewing about it until Pike says you're in the clear."

"I'm a worrier too, but I have a lot of confidence in Pike," Jack said.

"Georgie is on her way here now. I'll tell her that when she arrives."

"Please do, and I'll talk to her as well."

"I can usually calm her down," said Harry. "Plus she loves the Caledonia Steak House. Dinner will improve her mood."

"That's the place you're recommending for dinner?"

"It's the city's best steakhouse."

"Sounds good."

"Do you mind if we eat early? None of us slept well and we're all eager for an early night."

"Not at all."

"I'll book a table for six o'clock."

Jack poured another cup of coffee and carried it to the window. To his surprise, the sky was a clear blue with only a smattering of clouds. He had become so accustomed to the rain that he'd almost forgotten there were other types of Scottish weather.

"What are you thinking?" Anne said from behind him.

"Let's go for a walk. My body could use the exercise and it will help clear my head."

"You aren't going to work for a while? There's an envelope on the desk that was slid under the door last night. I imagine it's full of faxes from the office."

"The office can wait for a day. I want to go for a walk."

"Where do you want to go?"

"Nowhere in particular. Let's just roam. We'll explore the city on our own."

"That's a great idea. I'm ready any time you are," she said.

"I'll throw on some clothes. I can shower and shave when we get back."

Ten minutes later they left the hotel with a small pamphlet and a map. They walked along the Royal Mile, which ran just south of the Old Town. The area was well signed, and Jack and Anne debated where to start. Anne argued for the Greyfriars Kirkyard, which had been founded in 1560 and contained the graves of many distinguished Scots. Jack gave in to her. He had never understood Anne's fascination with cemeteries, but he followed along as she read the headstones.

They left the Kirkyard and walked uphill to the Old Town. The grey stone buildings that loomed over the narrow streets were as old as the graveyard. They stopped for coffee and then did some shopping for the grandchildren.

It was almost four o'clock when they left the Old Town. "We can walk another half mile or so down Holyrood Road to Holyrood Palace, or cross over and visit the National Museum," she said.

"We don't have enough time for a decent museum visit," Jack said.

"Holyrood is the Queen's official residence when she's in Scotland," Anne said. "We can do a quick tour."

Even with the quick tour, it was five o'clock when they got back to their room. The telephone light was blinking.

"I wonder who called," Anne said nervously.

Jack picked up the phone. There were two messages from Duncan Pike, half an hour apart. Both times he said simply, "This is Duncan Pike. Call me when you can."

"It was Pike. He called twice. He doesn't sound alarmed," Jack said, dialling the lawyer's number.

Pike answered the phone himself. "Jack, thank you for calling back so promptly," he said.

"Is something wrong?"

"No, it's actually very good news. Duff paid a visit to the police station at three this afternoon. He was accompanied by a lawyer who has a long-standing but unofficial relationship with my firm. Duff told Chief Inspector Henderson that the statement he gave last night was inaccurate. He said he'd had too much to drink and was confused, that things were clearer this morning and he wanted to set the record straight. He then put the blame squarely on McPherson for everything that transpired. The police were understandably skeptical and asked him several pointed questions, but according to the lawyer, Duff stood up well to them."

"That is very good news," Jack said.

"It will cost you about what I thought. Duff will get three thousand, another two hundred will go to the go-betweens, and the lawyer's fee is three hundred," Pike said. "The lawyer was a last-minute decision. I decided it would be too risky to depend on Duff alone; I wanted to be one hundred percent sure about what he actually told the police."

"The money isn't an issue," Jack said. "Again you have my thanks."

"We're still waiting on official word that no charges will be laid. I'm very confident that will be the case, but I suspect the police won't say anything until they have McPherson's medical report," said Pike. "I've asked a contact at the hospital to let me know when they send their report. You can be assured that I'll be on the phone with Henderson shortly thereafter."

Jack nodded at Anne, who was staring at him. "What a relief this is, Duncan. You've done a wonderful job."

Pike hesitated. "There's one other thing I need to tell you that isn't quite so wonderful."

"What is that?" Jack asked, immediately on edge.

"I got a call twenty minutes ago from a reporter with the *Glasgow Tribune*. The paper is a bit of a rag, a morning tabloid that peddles sensationalism. He asked me if I was representing you in relation to McPherson's death," Pike said. "I told him that I never discuss clients but I had heard rumblings that McPherson, a known felon, had dropped dead of a heart attack."

"How would they know about McPherson?"

"The paper has stringers at various police stations. For the price of a few pints they're given access to booking sheets and the like. I assume someone on the inside gave them your name and told them about McPherson."

"Should I be concerned about this?"

"Has anyone from the paper tried to contact you?"

"No."

"Then they probably won't. But if they do, I strongly suggest that you don't speak to them at all. They can take a simple 'no comment' and turn it into a one-act play."

"I'll follow your advice."

"Excellent. Now enjoy the rest of your evening. You'll hear from me again tomorrow, hopefully with positive news from our friends in the police force."

Jack hung up. Anne was still looking at him anxiously. "He gave me an update. Duff went to the police and changed his story. Pike thinks I should be officially off the hook tomorrow."

"Why did you ask him if you should be concerned?"

"He was contacted by a Glasgow newspaper asking questions about McPherson."

"What kind of questions?" she said, her anxiety even more apparent.

"Anne, I don't know what kind of questions, because Pike didn't let it get to that point," he said, now wishing he hadn't mentioned it. "As I said, Pike put them off."

"Still, a newspaper —"

"Forget about the newspaper. Pike made it clear their interest was in McPherson. The man had a criminal record and has been written about before. His name probably rang a bell," he said. "Now I need to get ready for dinner."

The sun had almost set and there was a nip in the air when they left the hotel. Anne shivered and pressed against Jack. The concierge's directions to the Caledonia Steak

House took them in the opposite direction from the Old Town. That meant an uphill walk into a light wind that stifled any conversation.

They reached the Angus exactly at six to find Harry, Barbara, and Georgie already there. Jack wasn't accustomed to being the last to arrive for anything. "Sorry for being on time," he said with a smile as he approached the table.

"Georgie came by the house and we left together," Harry said. "I had anticipated traffic that didn't materialize."

"I was joking," Jack said, and then held out his arms in Georgie's direction.

She came to her feet, wrapped her arms around his neck, and squeezed. "Did you get some sleep?" she asked.

"About eight hours," he said.

"Did you dream about him?" she asked.

"No, I didn't. Did you?" he said, noticing an urgency to her question.

"No, but I can't get him out of my head. I keep seeing his leering face."

"I'm not sure I'll ever stop seeing it," Jack said, and then stepped back to look at her. "Speaking of faces, how are you doing?"

"I'm okay, though I was so groggy when I woke that I quite forgot about my mouth. It was a bit of a shock when I looked in the mirror."

"The bottom lip doesn't look quite as swollen as it did last night," Anne said, leaving Barbara's arms to hug Georgie.

"It isn't, but the colour is godawful. Liz says a heavy coat of lipstick should help," Georgie said. "I have to do something, because I can't afford to take any more days off work."

As they sat down the waiter arrived with a drinks menu. Harry, Barbara, and Georgie already had theirs. Jack ordered a double Scotch and a gin martini for Anne.

"How was your day?" Jack asked Harry.

"Completely uneventful, thank God. And yours?"

"The same."

"That isn't exactly true," Anne said. "Duncan Pike called."

"You're smiling, Anne. Can we assume it was with good news?" asked Harry.

"Jack should tell you himself," she said.

"I was going to wait until things were absolutely certain," Jack said.

"That would be unfair," Georgie said.

Jack grimaced. "Well, all right, since I don't seem to have any choice. Pike said that McPherson's friend changed his story. He went to the police station with a lawyer and reversed his recounting of last night's events. He told them McPherson instigated the violence against Georgie and then threatened me."

"Which means the police aren't going to lay charges against Jack," Anne said.

"Pike wasn't quite that definite," Jack said.

"But he was close?" Georgie asked.

"Yes, he was close, but he didn't offer a guarantee."

"It would have been irresponsible if he had," Harry said. "Still, it all sounds very positive."

"It is, but I don't believe in taking things for granted. I don't want any celebrations until we know the outcome."

The waiter returned with the drinks for Anne and Jack. As soon as he had put them down, Harry raised his glass. "Here's to family."

After they had toasted, Jack looked around the table and felt a surge of emotion. "I'm so happy to have found you," he said.

"And we couldn't be happier that you did," Harry said.

An hour and a half later, Anne and Jack watched the others get into Harry's car and then walked downhill to their hotel, Anne clutching his arm again. She stumbled once or twice where the sidewalk was uneven. "Are you drunk?" he asked.

"Just a bit."

"That was a nice evening."

"Certainly better than last night."

"Let's not talk about that anymore," he said. "I was thinking again about inviting them to Wellesley. The summer would be a good time."

"We could do that, but I was also thinking it would be nice to bring the kids here to see where you were born and to meet everyone, and to support Liz at the Pitlochry Festival."

"We could do both."

"That would take up a lot of time. Are you thinking of retiring earlier than planned?"

"No, but we can work around my schedule."

"That would be a welcome change."

He stopped walking and looked at his wife. "Has our life really been that bad?"

"*Bad* is a word I'd never use," she said. "*Difficult*, however . . ."

"I know I can be difficult."

She smiled. "Whenever any of the children say that about you — and all of them have — I always tell them you're just more tightly focused than the rest of us."

He leaned down and kissed her gently on the lips. "I love you more than anything in my life."

"No, you don't, but it's enough that you love me as much as you do."

28

THEY MADE LOVE FOR the first time in ages that night, and afterwards they lay contentedly in each other's arms until Jack had to go to the bathroom. When he returned, Anne had put on her pajamas. He did the same and kissed her.

Jack got up twice during the night to use the washroom, and each time he had trouble getting back to sleep. Despite his confidence in Duncan Pike, there were still doubts in his mind that things would go as smoothly as the lawyer thought. He couldn't shake the idea that it was still possible for him to be charged with something. He knew it was unlikely, and he knew he wasn't being entirely logical. But he had no control over what was happening, and that was a situation he wasn't accustomed to.

At six Jack got out of bed and went into the living room. He ordered coffee from room service, retrieved the manila envelope that had been slid under the door, and put it under the one that had arrived the day before. He had two days of work to catch up on, and he was happy at the prospect. For the next couple of hours he read, annotated, and replied to the faxes sent by Pam. His attention was centred intensely on matters that—he reminded himself with a smile—were still his business.

It was almost eight o'clock when the phone rang. Jack was immersed in the summary of a report he'd requested on the pros and cons of acquiring a large regional insurance company in Denver. He didn't hear the phone until the third ring. "Jack Anderson," he answered.

"This is Harry."

Jack heard tension in his voice. "Has something happened?"

"It most definitely has. The *Glasgow Tribune* has a headline about McPherson splashed across its front page, and a story about us on the second page."

"What does it say?" Jack said through clenched teeth.

"I don't want to read it to you," Harry said, his voice shaking. "You need to see it for yourself. They'll have a copy at the hotel."

"Pike said the paper was snooping around. They called him yesterday but he wouldn't talk to them. He told me the paper is a rag."

"You didn't mention that to us last night."

"Pike made nothing of it, so I didn't think it was important."

"Well, Pike was wrong to ignore them. The paper is a rag, all right, but while it isn't *The Scotsman* or *The Times* of London, it is one of the most widely read papers in the country."

"I had a hunch things weren't going to run as smoothly as Pike thought."

"Jack, please, do me a favour," Harry said. "Go downstairs, buy the newspaper, and then call me right back."

"I'll do that," Jack said, putting down the phone. The cold sweat had returned, and he had a lump in his stomach the size of a tennis ball. He tried to collect himself, but his mind was jumping in ten different directions. He knew he had to read the paper. He reached for the phone again and called the concierge. "Could you bring two copies of this morning's *Glasgow Tribune* to my room," he said. "Do it right away, please."

I should get dressed, he thought. *But I'd probably wake Anne, and I'd rather see what I'm dealing with first. How bad can it be? What can they have written about us?*

He sat impatiently at the desk for a couple of minutes, then stood and went to the room door. He watched the elevators through the eyehole. Finally one stopped at the floor and a bellboy stepped out, carrying two newspapers. Jack opened the door and held out his hand. "Thank you. I don't have any cash on me right now. I'll give you a tip later in the day," he said as he took the papers.

He carried them to the desk and sat. The *Tribune* was a tabloid. Its front page that morning had a banner across the top that read "RANGERS VERSUS CELTIC PREDICTIONS." Across the bottom another banner read "TORY

POLITICIAN'S LOVE NEST FUNDED BY PUBLIC MONEY."
The rest of the page was taken up by two stories. On the
left side, accompanied by a large photo of a burning building, was the headline "DOCKSIDE WAREHOUSE GOES UP
IN FLAMES — ARSON SUSPECTED." On the right were
two smaller photos. One was the old shot of McPherson
that Georgie had found; the other was of Jack. It was a
corporate photo that went into the annual reports and was
used by the company's publicity team. Under the photo
the caption read, "'Bloody' Jack Anderson." Jack read the
headline, "SHOCK OF FAMILY REUNION WITH MILLION-
AIRE YANK SON KILLS ELDERLY GLASWEGIAN, *See full
story on page 2.*"

The knot in Jack's stomach tightened as he turned the
page and began to read.

American multi-millionaire and insurance business
tycoon 'Bloody' Jack Anderson came to Scotland
less than a week ago to look for long-lost family
members. Among others, he found his father, Douglas
McPherson, an eighty-two-year-old Glaswegian he
hadn't seen in over fifty years. Hours later McPherson
was dead and the police are asking questions.

Mr. Anderson, the CEO of Pilgrim Insurance of
Boston, was born in Scotland but was adopted and
sent to America when he was a boy. He returned to this
country to visit a sister, Moira, who lives in Irvine, and
that in turn led him to a brother, Harry Montgomery

of Edinburgh, and a second sister, Georgina Malcolm, also of Edinburgh. Mrs. Malcolm was formerly of Bearsden and is the wife of the alleged investment fund swindler Atholl Malcolm. She was never implicated in any of her husband's dealings.

Mr. Anderson did not know of his father's existence until he arrived in Scotland. When he discovered it, he, Mr. Montgomery and Mrs. Malcolm decided to track him down.

Mr. McPherson had led a troubled life. In the 1960s he was convicted of manslaughter after killing a man in a pub brawl, and while in jail he killed another inmate and received an additional sentence. But since his release from prison, McPherson had an unblemished record and, according to friends, was enjoying a peaceful retirement. On Thursday night past that peace was shattered.

On that night, Mr. Anderson, Mrs. Malcolm, and Mr. Montgomery went to the Tartan Rover pub in the Gorbals. They knew Mr. McPherson frequented the pub and had been told beforehand that he was on the premises. They found him there and without warning they confronted him.

Witnesses say Mr. McPherson reacted poorly to the surprise and took particular umbrage with Mrs. Malcolm. They had a short, angry exchange. Hands were raised, and at that point witnesses say Mr. Anderson became involved. Seconds later, Mr. McPherson fell to the floor. He was later declared dead at Glasgow Infirmary.

The Strathclyde Police have not laid any charges, but Mr. Anderson was held overnight for questioning. Mr. Anderson's lawyer, Duncan Pike, declined our request for an interview.

Speaking for the Strathclyde Police, CI Arthur Henderson said, 'This was a series of tragic events. First reports are that Mr. McPherson died of a heart attack, but we have no way of knowing what caused it. We are carefully reviewing what went on at the pub, and we'll make a decision in the next few days as to whether further steps need to be taken. All we can say is that it is a sad day when the reunion of a father with his children ends in such a tragic manner.'

"Fuck!" Jack shouted.

"Fuck what?" Anne said from the bedroom.

He handed her the newspaper. "Read this. I have to call Duncan Pike. I only hope he's working on a Saturday morning."

Anne frowned, looked at the front page, and gasped.

Jack dialled the number for Pike. When he heard a woman answer, he said, "This is Jack Anderson. I need to speak to Duncan."

"One moment, please."

"Good morning, Jack. I imagine you're calling about the *Tribune*," Pike said, almost exactly a second later.

"I am. What kind of garbage is this?"

"It's exactly the kind of garbage the *Tribune* specializes in, and our best course of action is to ignore it completely."

"You don't think other newspapers will pick it up?"

"Given your involvement, it's possible the financial press might give it a mention, but I'm sure it would be no more than a snippet."

"I don't want any snippets."

"I understand that, but it's out of our control."

Jack stared at the article. "The story is filled with innuendo. It makes it seem as if I had something to do with his death. It implies that you're ducking questions and that the police are trying to figure out what they can charge me with. This is not what I expected when I spoke to you last night."

"That's how the *Tribune* operates. They were careful to ensure that nothing they've published is actually libellous. And any effort on our part to clarify or correct the record will only extend the story's life," Pike said. "If we say nothing and do nothing, it will die a natural death."

Despite his roiling emotions, Jack saw the logic in Pike's position. "The other thing that angers me is the police had to be the primary source for this. I mean, all those details could only come from one place."

"I have zero doubt that the police were the source. But that isn't necessarily a bad thing," Pike said. "In fact, I think it could be a very good thing."

"How so?"

"I suspect that Henderson was considering bringing

an assault charge against you. I don't think in the end he would have, but Duff's revised statement took the decision out of his hands," Pike said. "Henderson likely suspects we got to Duff, and I'm guessing that annoyed him enough that he decided to embarrass you by going to the *Tribune*. In the process I think he's sending a very clear signal that there won't be any charges."

"Are you certain?"

"Absolutely."

"Then why don't I feel better?"

"Anyone would be upset at having their picture splashed across the front page of a paper like the *Tribune*," Pike said. "But by tomorrow morning there'll be a different picture and you'll be forgotten."

"So you want me to do nothing?"

"Exactly. I want you to say and do absolutely nothing," Pike said. "Ignore the *Tribune*, don't take calls from any other media, and don't fret about what the police will do."

"Well, I'll try."

"I'm sure you'll do just fine, but if you have any further doubts, I'm here."

"Thank you," Jack said, and ended the conversation.

Anne stared at him from the sofa. Her face was pale and her mouth sagged. "What did he say?"

"He said to say and do nothing, that it will all pass in a day," Jack said. "He also told me he's sure no charges will be laid against me. That story in the *Tribune* is the police's way of taking revenge on us for turning Duff."

"Then it isn't nearly as bad as this story looks?"

"That's what Pike insists."

"Then why are you so down?"

Jack picked up the newspaper. "I'm not used to things like this. I've spent my entire career building a reputation as someone who is responsible and dependable. This story makes me look unhinged. I mean, what kind of man springs that kind of news on an eighty-two-year-old and then ends up involved in his death?"

"I don't think this will hurt your reputation, if that's your main worry," Anne said. "There's a perfectly good explanation, after all, and your friends and business acquaintances know what kind of man you really are. They'll give you the benefit of any doubt."

"Don't be so sure about that," Jack said. "I do have enemies, both inside and outside Pilgrim. A lot of people would love to see Jack Anderson get knocked off his high horse. This story could provide them with ammunition."

"Even if you're right—and I don't think you are—what are the chances that people back home will see this story?" Anne said. "It's a Glasgow tabloid, for goodness' sake. And Pike did say it would be a one-day item."

"I'd like to believe no one at home will see this, but I can't count on it. The question is, should we give our family and friends and my board a heads-up?"

"The moment we do that, they'll go looking for the story. Then who knows who they'll talk to, and so on and so on. You could make things worse," Anne said. "If Pike says it will be history by tomorrow, then we should trust his judgement and ignore it."

"I'm afraid that my board will hear about this from someone other than me."

"What if they do? You have an explanation. You've done nothing wrong. Pike says there won't be any charges."

"Even if I've done nothing illegal, it's still rather lurid. It could call my judgement into question."

"What does it matter what the board thinks?" Anne said. "You've already resigned. Are you afraid they'll ask you to make an early exit?"

Jack closed his eyes and shook his head. Was this the time to tell her? Nothing was definite. Why muddy the waters even more? "I'm not convinced that trying to ride this out is the best approach, but you're right, the other option has its own set of pitfalls," he said, and smiled wanly.

"I think Pike understands this better than us. Let's listen to him."

Jack nodded. "He could be right. Maybe the story will die a natural death. After the past few days I figure I'm owed some luck," he said. "Now, I promised Harry I'd call him back."

Anne sighed. "Call Harry, but don't make any plans with him or Georgie for today. You and I will spend it together. Another good long walk is what we need," she said. "We'll have dinner with them if you want, but I just think we need some time together."

29

THEY SPENT THE MORNING walking through the Old Town again, and after lunch they visited the National Museum of Scotland.

Anne chatted a good deal of the time. Jack listened but didn't really hear. He couldn't shake his thoughts about the *Tribune* story and continued to be torn about his decision not to notify Pilgrim. He checked his watch constantly, taking five hours off Edinburgh time and conjuring mental images of activity at the office. Since becoming president, he had made a practice of going to the office on a Saturday morning so he could tie up the week's loose ends and prepare for the coming one. Most other members of the executive team and their key staff followed his lead. So unless his absence from the office had dramatically changed everyone's work habits, he imagined Pam would be arriving soon to sort the overnight faxes and mail. Norman Gordon would arrive shortly thereafter.

His office was separated from Jack's by Pam's, and most Saturday mornings he'd walk over to Jack's to compare notes on the week. *With me not there, I wonder who he'll talk to, and what the subject of conversation is going to be? Could it be me?* Jack wondered.

The longer the day went on in Edinburgh, the more Jack thought he had made a mistake by not contacting Don Arnold or Ross Goldsmith. He should also have warned Pam. Anne had made some good points, but he was becoming convinced that he had let his emotions over-rule his common sense. Was it just wishful thinking to believe that the *Tribune* story wouldn't find its way across the Atlantic? Nothing travelled faster than bad news. By three o'clock he'd decided he had to know if his bad news had travelled to Boston.

"I want to go back to the hotel," he said abruptly to Anne as they stood in front of a Robert the Bruce exhibit at the museum. "It's already ten in the morning at home, and I want to know if things are quiet."

"I'm sure they will be."

"I keep thinking I was unrealistic to hope that story could be contained here."

"We'll go back to the hotel," Anne said.

"No arguments?"

"You've got that look on your face that tells me I'd be wasting my breath."

Anne had to hurry to keep up with him on the return walk. When they reached their suite, he unlocked the door and went in ahead of her. She looked past him and saw the message light on the phone blinking. "Maybe Harry or Georgie called," she said.

Jack picked up the phone and accessed his calls. Anne watched him closely. His face was grim, and she suspected there was more than one message. "Well?" she said when he finally put down the receiver.

"So much for wishful thinking," he said. "There are two messages from Pam asking me to call her. Ross Goldsmith also called twice, saying he needs to talk to me. He sounded distant. Don Arnold wants to talk to me. Norman Gordon said he was just touching base and if there's anything he can do to help, all I have to do is ask."

"I guess the *Glasgow Tribune* has a wider readership than Duncan Pike believes," she said.

He tapped the middle finger of his right hand on the desk as he thought about whom to call first. Then it struck him that they hadn't heard from any of the children. "Anne, I suspect I'm going to be tied up here for a while, but it just dawned on me that the children probably don't know what's going on. Let's not leave it to strangers to tell them. Why don't you go downstairs and call them." He was about to add *don't alarm them* but ate his words. Anne knew better than he did how to talk to the kids.

"That's a very good idea," she said.

"Before you do, though, let me phone Duncan Pike. He might have an update from the police."

"I'll go to the bathroom while you do."

He dialled Pike's office and was put on hold. Three minutes later he was still on hold and getting agitated when the receptionist came back on the line. "Mr. Pike apologizes for the delay. He'll be right with you," she said.

"Jack, your timing is impeccable," Pike said a few seconds later.

"How so?"

"I was on the other line with Superintendent Gillespie of the Strathclyde Police. Glasgow is part of the Greater Strathclyde jurisdiction and Chief Inspector Henderson reports to Gillespie. He had kicked your case upstairs for a final decision. Fortunately Gillespie and I are on very good terms, so I was able to speak to the man directly," Pike said. "He just informed me that the medical report says McPherson died of a heart attack, and that his heart was in such poor condition it was a wonder he hadn't died years ago."

"So no charges?"

"No charges. Duff's statement made it clear that McPherson initiated whatever violence occurred, and not even the most zealous of prosecutors could justify charging a man for coming to the rescue of his sister," Pike said. "That last phrase is a direct quote from the superintendent."

"That's a relief, though I have to say this *Tribune* story has put a sour edge to it."

"Forget the *Tribune*."

"Will the police issue any kind of statement saying that I've been cleared?"

"You were never charged, so technically there's nothing to clear. And they don't normally put out statements about the outcomes of pub brawls. If they did, they'd have to enlarge their staff."

"I understand that, but I have associates in the U.S. who might need to be reassured that I'm blameless in all this."

"I'll speak to them if you wish," said Pike.

"You're my lawyer, so you're hardly neutral. Would the superintendent talk to them?"

"Who exactly do you have in mind?"

"The chairman of my board, and maybe the vice-chair."

"That might be arranged."

"Thank you. I'll let you know if they request that," Jack said. "Now you and I have a bill we need to settle."

"I'll send it to the hotel."

"I'll make arrangements to have it paid before I leave Scotland."

"Excellent. Well, I have to say it's been enjoyable doing business with you, but hopefully our paths will never cross again."

"Amen to that," Jack said, and ended the call.

"Amen to what?" Anne asked from the bathroom door, where she'd been listening to his conversation.

"There will be no charges. The medical report confirms that McPherson had a bad heart that caused his death. The police have determined that he initiated the violence and I was simply and naturally defending my sister. Pike even thinks he might be able to get the police superintendent to affirm that to my board."

"That's wonderful!"

"And now you have something definite to tell the children."

"I already had something definite. They don't know yet that they have an uncle, another aunt, and three cousins over here."

Jack shook his head. "What a week."

"And it isn't over yet," Anne said, walking over to the desk. She put her arms around her husband's neck and kissed him. "Call your chairman and calm him down. I'll let the kids know that you're okay and that our family has just doubled in size."

Jack waited until Anne closed the door behind her before reaching for the phone. He called his direct line. "Mr. Anderson's office," Pam answered.

"It's me," he said.

"Oh, sir, I'm so glad to hear from you. It's been crazy here this morning."

"I meant to call earlier, but I had some family business to attend to," he said, as low-key as he could manage. "What's going on?"

"A story in a Glasgow newspaper about you and your father."

"How did you learn about it?"

"Several copies were sent to your fax machine. And then Mr. Gordon brought a copy to the office," she said.

She hesitated before adding, "The story is everywhere, Mr. Anderson. I've taken calls from board members, the news media, and colleagues from Pilgrim and other companies. I've kept a list of those I thought were most important. Do you want me to read it to you?"

"That's not necessary. Mr. Arnold and Mr. Goldsmith phoned me here. I'll return their calls as soon as you and I are done."

"And Mr. Gordon really wants to speak to you."

"I have to talk to the chairman and vice-chairman first."

"Yes, sir."

"Pam, I need you to take down a statement that I want you to release through our internal system. You have approval on my authority."

"Yes, sir," she said, without the conviction he would have liked to hear.

"Write this down," he said.

"Do you want it sent as a message from the president?"

"Yes, I think that would be appropriate, since I still have the job," he said sardonically.

"I'm ready, sir."

"A newspaper story concerning me, published today in the *Glasgow Tribune*, requires some explanation and clarification," he began. "I am currently in Scotland and have been for most of the past week. I came here to trace my family roots. In the process, I discovered that I have a brother and sister previously unknown to me. We connected in the most positive manner and I'm convinced our relationship will now be ongoing. Finding them has been a blessing to me and my family.

"I also discovered to my surprise that my biological father, the man who put me up for adoption more than fifty years ago, was still alive. He had a violent checkered past and my new-found siblings and I debated whether we should try to locate him. We decided we should and were successful. In retrospect, that wasn't wise, because when we met him, he became violent and attacked my sister. He then suffered a heart attack and died shortly thereafter in hospital. Official medical reports have confirmed that he had a long-standing heart condition.

"The local police carried out an extensive investigation and found me and my siblings blameless in my father's death. No charges will be laid. The fact that the *Tribune*—a tabloid newspaper with a reputation for sensationalism—chose to print a story about our family situation is unfortunate, but it was beyond my control. I regret any embarrassment this incident may have caused Pilgrim and expect to be back at my desk next week fulfilling my responsibilities.

"How does that sound to you, Pam?" he asked.

"It certainly explains a great many things," she said after a slight hesitation.

"Good. Then put my name on it and send it out."

"Yes, sir. Shall I tell Mr. Gordon you called?"

"That isn't necessary. I'll phone him after I've spoken with Mr. Arnold and Mr. Goldsmith."

Taking at least partial control of the situation had given Jack the first trace of relief he'd experienced since Harry's phone call that morning. But he knew the next call would tell him if the relief was justified.

"Mr. Goldsmith's office," the receptionist said.

"This is Jack Anderson calling for Mr. Goldsmith," he said.

"He's been expecting your call, sir. Just one minute," she said.

Jack took a deep breath. He was taking nothing for granted with Goldsmith.

"Jack, what's going on over there?" Goldsmith barked. "Both Boston papers, the *New York Times,* the *Wall Street Journal,* and God knows how many other news media have called Don and me asking for comments about the story in that Scottish newspaper. Do you know how embarrassing it is to have to say 'no comment' about a story that directly involves our CEO?"

"Nothing has occurred that should cause you or the board any concern," Jack said as his cold sweat returned. "And I apologize for not reaching out to you sooner. I was waiting until I heard from my lawyer so I could give you the entire story. I just spoke to him, and everything is now crystal clear and trouble-free at this end."

"It's a bit late for an explanation, let alone an apology."

"Ross, I've just finished dictating to Pam an internal communication that explains in detail what happened—"

"Has she sent it?" Goldsmith interrupted.

"She's preparing it now."

"I don't want her to send anything out until Don and I have approved it."

"Ross, the last time I looked, I was still president of this company."

"That may be true, but Don and I have an equal responsibility to protect Pilgrim's reputation."

"The story is bullshit," Jack said. "Listen, call Pam, get her to read my statement to you, and then call me back. If you have any questions, I'll answer them in full."

"I'll do that, but I hope you understand how unhappy we are to be caught off guard like this," Goldsmith said. "The very first thing Don said to me was 'Why didn't we hear about this from Jack?'"

"I wasn't about to wake you at three o'clock in the morning to tell you about a bullshit story," he said. "I should have called before now, I admit, but I wanted to hear from the lawyer. It isn't as if I'm a day late."

Goldsmith went quiet, and Jack suspected he hadn't blunted his response as well as he needed to.

"I'll phone Pam," Goldsmith said finally. "Then I'll get back to you. Don't do anything until I do."

Jack thought about phoning Don Arnold but decided to wait to hear from Goldsmith. It took thirty minutes before he called back, and Jack knew his vice-chairman had done more than talk to Pam.

"I sent your statement to Don," Goldsmith said first. "We went over it together, and it does start to clarify matters."

"My lawyer in Glasgow can set up a conversation between you and the superintendent of police if that will add to your comfort level," Jack said.

"There's no need for that."

"So can we put this behind us?"

"I believe I can, but Don isn't entirely comfortable with things as they stand."

"Ross, I did nothing wrong."

"Perhaps not, but the perception is less than ideal."

"How can I convince him there's no need to worry?"

"If he'd heard about this directly from you, he might be more receptive to your explanation. As it is, he feels you were hoping the story wouldn't get further than Glasgow. He thinks you were trying to hide it from us."

"I'll call him."

"I wouldn't bother doing that today; he's not going to be listening very well. It might be best to leave things as they are until you get back here and we three can have a sit-down."

"Is this going to affect my tenure at Pilgrim?"

"No. We discussed that."

"Thank you."

"Jack, don't leap to conclusions," Goldsmith said. "All I mean is that we agreed you should serve out the rest of your term to retirement. Frankly, there's no chance now that the board will agree to an extension."

"Just a second," Jack said loudly. "Why should this change anything? Are you telling me that a bogus story in a Scottish tabloid kills our agreement?"

"For the record, there was no agreement. What we had was an understanding that the board would reconsider your retirement date."

"And now?"

"The way you've handled this has eroded Don's confidence in you. He was never completely sold on extending your tenure. Now he'll oppose it if it comes before the board, and without Don, it won't pass. You should forget the entire notion, Jack. And if you do decide to pursue it, you'll have to get another board member to make the proposal for you. I can't do it now," Goldsmith said.

"Going to the board without support from you and Don is pointless."

"I agree, but I'm not telling you what to do."

"I expected better than this from you, Ross."

"And I expected better from you," Goldsmith said. "I think you should be grateful that we'll continue to support you both within the company and publicly, and that we're committed to maintaining the status quo."

"That's no less than I deserve."

"I agree, but I have to tell you, if anything new emerges about your exploits in Scotland, even the status quo will not be sustainable. So if there's anything you haven't told me, now is the time."

"There's nothing," Jack snapped.

"Good," Goldsmith said.

"And I want to have a meeting with you and Don when I get back."

"That can be arranged. Neither of us is taking any pleasure in this. We still respect everything you've done for Pilgrim," Goldsmith said. "And I think, when you take the time to consider our position, you'll agree that we're being fair and reasonable."

"I'll see you next week," Jack said, and put down the phone.

Jack poured a Scotch, set down the bottle, and put his feet up on the coffee table. He gulped down the drink and poured another. The knot in his stomach unravelled, the warmth of the liquor deadening his senses as its tendrils spread through his body.

I'm finished, he thought. One lapse in judgement and just like that, he was gone. Goldsmith had said they were going to let him finish his term, but he knew that for the next five months that was the very best he could expect. If he were younger they might have let the issue slide and given him a chance to rebuild trust. But there was no benefit in doing that for a man who had such a short shelf life.

Would they want him to retire early? When he met with Goldsmith and Arnold in Boston, they might raise the subject — as a suggestion, of course, not as a demand. There was nothing to be gained by insulting him. They would want him to work with Gordon to make the transition as smooth as possible and then go quietly. He knew it would be stupid of him not to; his employment contract contained a morals clause that included a provision for its termination if his behaviour brought the company into public disrepute. He wondered if a termination would also affect his pension, and suspected it might.

He poured a third Scotch and swore at himself. As much as he wanted to believe they were being unreasonable, he knew he had made a mistake by not calling them sooner. If someone who worked for him had failed to tell him about something that was potentially impactful, he would have been irate. Why should he expect two seasoned board members like Goldsmith and Arnold to act any differently?

"Calm down. You're overreacting," he muttered to himself. Goldsmith had said that Arnold was initially resistant to extending his term. If that was true — and he didn't doubt Goldsmith — then the story by itself would have been enough to scupper the extension. And nothing had changed where Anne, the kids, and his staff at Pilgrim were concerned. As far as they knew, he was leaving as planned. In a few months the *Tribune* story would become a faded memory and he'd leave the company with his pride and reputation more or less intact.

"Jack, is everything okay? Your face is really flushed," Anne said.

He hadn't noticed her come into the suite. "You surprised me."

"And you're drinking already. Were your talks with Ross and Don that bad?"

"I only spoke to Ross, and it was fine."

"Really?"

"Well, he was a bit upset that I hadn't called him sooner. He didn't like finding out second-hand."

"Oh, Jack, I'm so sorry," she said. "I shouldn't have interfered. I should have stayed quiet and let you follow your instincts."

"There's no point in second-guessing. Besides, you didn't hold a gun to my head, and I don't think it would have made any real difference if I'd called earlier."

"What are they going to do?"

"Nothing."

"Nothing at all?"

"I'm releasing a statement that will go to all of our employees and associates. I'm sure it will also be sent to the business press at home. Other than that, nothing changes. I'll go back and run the company until my retirement."

"That was very understanding of them."

"After everything I've done for that company . . ."

Anne looked at the bottle on the table. "You've had quite a bit to drink."

"Not that much."

"Maybe we should stay in tonight."

"I have to eat," he said, and then suddenly remembered why she had been gone. "Did you reach the children?"

"I spoke to Brent and Mark and left a message for Allison. The boys had heard about what happened, and they are very worried about you. Brent said he knows some good lawyers in the U.K. if you need one. Mark offered to fly over."

"They'd heard that soon?"

"They said the story is the talk of the financial community."

"In hindsight, that was to be expected."

"Do I need to say I'm sorry again?" Anne asked.

"Of course not. The truth is, it was my decision. I might have made the same one without your advice. To be honest, I knew the story would spread, but I was clinging to the hope that it wouldn't," Jack said. "It wasn't realistic, but I didn't like the alternative. So I took the chance."

"But you said the talk with Ross went fine, so what difference did it make?"

"They'll look at me a bit differently, that's all," he said. "In all my years at the company I've never put a foot wrong, at least not that anyone knows about. Now I have, and I have to say it's eating at me."

"What does that matter? You'll be gone soon enough. Let Norman Gordon worry about the board."

Jack nodded and poured himself another Scotch. "You haven't said yet how the kids reacted to the news about their new family?"

"They're pleased if you're pleased, but really they were far more concerned about what's happening to their father. We can revisit the story about our new family members when we get home and things are calmer."

The phone rang. Anne stared at it. "That could be Allison," she said as she crossed the floor. She picked it up, listened, and then passed the phone to Jack. "It's Harry. He sounds very upset."

"What now?" Jack said, pulling himself to his feet. He walked over to Anne and took the phone from her. "What's going on? Do we have another news article to worry about?"

"I wish we did," Harry said. "Georgie is here. She's had a visit from one of the Baxter boys. We need to talk."

30

JACK AND ANNE TOOK a taxi to Harry's house, unsure of what they were going to find there. Harry hadn't wanted to go into detail over the phone and kept insisting they come as soon as possible.

Perhaps because he'd had almost four Scotches, Jack didn't seem panicked by the request. But Anne was alarmed and asked him five times during the taxi ride what he thought was behind it. His reply — "I have no idea, and let's not leap to conclusions" — did nothing to calm her. When they finally reached the house, her anxiety level was through the roof.

Harry opened the door before they reached it, his face haggard. When Anne hugged him, she felt a tremor of fear. "Where's Georgie?" she asked, looking behind him into the empty hallway.

"She's upstairs with Barbara. They'll be down in a minute," Harry said.

They went into the living room. "Drinks?" Harry asked as they sat down.

"I'll have a Scotch," said Jack.

"Nothing for me," Anne said, and then added quickly, "What's going on?"

"Billy Baxter and one of his goons paid Georgie a visit," Harry said.

Anne heard a noise from the stairway and saw Barbara holding Georgie by the hand as she helped her navigate the last few steps. Anne went to the door to meet them. As she got closer, she saw that Georgie's eyes were filled with tears and her right cheek was gashed and bloody.

"Oh my god!" Anne said. "What did they do to you?"

"Billy Baxter hit me," Georgie said. "He slapped me with the back of his hand. His ring cut me."

"Have you called the police?" Anne asked Barbara.

"No. Georgie doesn't want us to."

"Georgie, why on earth not?" Anne said.

"It would just make things worse."

"But you need protection."

"The police protecting me from the Baxters? That's not on. If the Baxters decide they want to harm me, then one way or another they will," Georgie said.

"But why?" Anne asked.

Georgie looked across the coffee table at Jack and shuddered.

"They want money," Harry said.

An uncomfortable silence fell over the room. The women sat down.

"Should I assume that the money they want would come from me?" Jack said.

"Yes, that's their plan," said Harry.

Jack sipped his Scotch and shook his head slowly. "What else do I need to know?"

"I don't want you to do anything," Georgie blurted, tears coursing down her cheeks. "It isn't right. This has nothing to do with you."

Harry reached for his sister, his hand resting gently on her knee. "Georgie, like it or not, the Baxters have brought Jack into this. He has a right to know what was said."

"Yes, tell me, please," Jack said.

"You tell him. I can't," Georgie said to Harry.

Harry sipped his drink and licked his lips. He didn't look at Jack as he said, "They want money. They saw the story in the *Tribune* this morning and figured that now Georgie has a wealthy American brother, you should pony up some of the money stolen by Atholl."

"There is a twisted logic behind that," said Jack. "How much do they want?"

"They didn't say. They want to speak to you directly," Georgie said.

"And if I refuse, what happens then?"

"They'll pay Georgie another visit. Only this time, they said, they wouldn't go so easy on her," Harry said. "They also mentioned Liz, and I wouldn't put it past them to hurt her."

"Animals," Anne said.

"I'm embarrassed that they're Scots," Harry said.

"Embarrassed or not, we can't ignore them," Jack said.

"I don't want you paying them any money," Georgie said.

"I haven't said I will," Jack said. "Do they know where I'm staying?"

"I didn't tell them."

"Do you have a phone number for this Billy Baxter?"

"It's upstairs in my handbag."

"Did he set a deadline?"

"He said if he doesn't hear from you within twenty-four hours, he'll assume your answer is no."

"Someone please get me the phone number," Jack said.

"I'll go," Barbara said.

Jack watched her leave and felt Anne's and Harry's eyes on him. His mind was sluggish from the liquor he'd consumed and the emotional turmoil of the day. He hoped no one would ask him what he was going to do, because he had no idea.

Georgie rested her head against the back of the sofa, the glare from the overhead lights highlighting her face and making the gash on her cheek look even more grue-some. Anne held her hand and muttered, "Things will be okay, you'll see."

When Barbara returned, Jack took the crumpled piece of paper with Baxter's number. "We should get going," he said to Anne.

She looked up at him, surprised.

He leaned over and kissed Georgie on the forehead. "I'll call this Billy Baxter," he said.

"Don't give him any money," she urged.

"I'll call him," Jack repeated.

"Do you want a drive back to the hotel?" Harry asked.

"Yes, that would be good," said Jack.

After a round of uncomfortable goodbyes, Anne and Jack left with Harry. The car was no sooner on the road when Harry asked, "What are you going to do?"

"I don't know yet. I'd appreciate a little quiet, though," Jack said wearily. "I need to think."

31

JACK DIDN'T SPEAK AGAIN until the car stopped in front of the hotel, and then all he said was "I'll be in touch."

"What are you going to do?" Anne asked as they walked through the lobby.

"I'm still thinking," he said, checking his watch.

"You have to help her," Anne said.

He didn't reply as they got into the elevator. When they reached their floor, he exited quickly and went ahead to their suite. He walked directly to the desk, picked up the phone, and started to dial.

"Are you calling Billy Baxter?" she asked from the doorway.

Jack shook his head and said, "Duncan, I'm glad I caught you. I hope it isn't too late."

"Many of my clients work irregular hours. I try to accommodate them. What can I do for you?"

"As it turns out, I may need your services again."

"Then it's a good thing I haven't yet sent you my bill," Pike said. Then he caught himself. "I don't mean to make light of your reason for calling."

"The situation I'm calling about stems directly from the *Tribune* story that ran this morning," Jack said. "One of your Glasgow gangs read the story and decided to try a little extortion."

"That sounds odd."

"If you remember, the paper mentioned that my sister Georgie's husband is Atholl Malcolm. Evidently the Baxter boys were among the victims of his financial scam. I'm sure you know who they are."

"I do indeed. They've been clients of mine," Pike said. "And of course I did hear rumblings that Malcolm left the country with a large sum of their money."

"I don't know if he did or not, but I do know they're demanding that I repay what they claim he took," Jack said. "They visited my sister months ago to ask about Malcolm's whereabouts and see what money they could squeeze out of her. Since she has no idea where he is and he left her high and dry, they let her be. They visited her again today and demanded that her new-found wealthy American brother make good on their losses — or else."

"Yes, with the Baxters there's always an 'or else,'" Pike said. "Did they hurt her?"

"Yes, they bloodied her face. They've promised to do even worse if I don't pay, and they hinted that Georgie's daughter, Liz, could be targeted as well."

"They are a crude bunch," Pike said. "Which of the Baxters visited your sister?"

"Billy."

"He's the youngest and the most prone to violence. He has three older brothers who have mellowed somewhat over the years. They aren't saints, mind you, but they take a more balanced approach to business."

"Then I would like you to speak to one of the older brothers on my behalf," Jack said.

"Assuming I can find one agreeable to a conversation, what do you want me to say?"

"I want them to lay off Georgie and Liz."

"Of course you do. And what will you offer them in return?"

"We won't report to the police their attempt at extortion or the violence against Georgie."

"Jack, I don't mean to sound dismissive, but you should know that the Baxters are not the type to worry about the police," Pike said, and paused. "Would you object to my being completely candid with you?"

"Of course not."

"Well, I have to tell you that your idea has virtually no merit. In fact it's more likely to offend the Baxters and probably hurt rather than help your sister," said Pike. "When you fly off to America, Georgie will be left here by herself to deal with them. We don't want to make it worse for her than it already is."

Anne was sitting in a chair across from Jack as he spoke

to Pike. Her eyes never left his face. Jack turned his head slightly to avoid her stare. "Okay, if going to the police is not an option, let me ask you some questions," he said. "If I refuse to pay the extortion money, do you believe the Baxters will follow through on their threats to harm Georgie and her daughter?"

"I can't say for certain, but I wouldn't put it past them. There would definitely be the risk."

"Is there any way of assessing that risk? Could you talk to one of the older brothers and feel him out?"

"Jack, you can't approach the Baxters as if they were some kind of actuarial problem. This isn't the insurance business," Pike said. "I think the risk is real, but I can't possibly assess to what extent."

"Okay, then tell me, if I did pay them something, how could I be sure they wouldn't come back looking for more money six months from now?"

"How much is something?"

"I don't know. They didn't give Georgie a number. Billy wants me to call him. I assume there'll be some kind of negotiation."

"Are you prepared to speak to Billy?"

"No. I thought I'd made that clear. If there's going to be any negotiation, I want you to represent me," Jack said. "Are you prepared to do that?"

"I am, and I have to say that's a rather wise decision on your part."

"That will depend on the outcome," Jack said. "And

you didn't answer my question about them honouring a deal."

"On balance, I think they might, but I wouldn't take their word for it. I would insist on a written contract."

"Are you serious?"

"Absolutely. Given the nature of their relationship with Atholl Malcolm and the debt he owes, we could construct something that says Georgie is paying them a portion of it and in exchange they absolve her of any further responsibility for the balance. It would not look like extortion from their end and it would free your sister from any future obligation. It could be a win-win."

"Except for the fact that I have to put up the money."

"Aye, there is that."

"And you believe they'd honour a written contract?"

"I can construct something with enough legal hooks that they'd have no choice."

Jack put his elbows on the desk and rubbed his face with his free hand. He thought about his options and didn't like any of them.

"Jack, are you still on the line?" Pike asked.

"I've been thinking," he said. "I've decided that you should call the Baxters. Find out how much they want and try to determine if they'll settle for less."

"I can do that."

"They also have to agree to your contract proposal."

"I'll call Mark; he's the eldest. At the end of the day he'll be the one making the decision for the family."

"I'll be here. Call me when you have some answers," Jack said, and hung up.

Anne rose from her chair and crossed the room. She stood behind him and wrapped her arms around him. "I knew you would help," she said. "I'm proud of you."

"I haven't agreed to anything," he said. "Pike is going to call the Baxters. We don't know what they want, and until we do, it's impossible to say how this will end."

"But you've taken the first step," she said. "What happens now?"

"We wait for Pike to call back."

"How long will that take?"

"I don't know."

"I'm a nervous wreck," Anne said. "I can only imagine what Georgie is going through."

"I imagine she's more experienced at handling this kind of stress than we are."

"That isn't the impression I got."

"All I'm saying is that I think she's tougher than she's letting on."

"Is that an indirect way of warning me that you might not help her?"

"No. But you can't take it for granted that we'll be able to help. All I can do is wait to hear from Duncan Pike."

"What I want to do is lie down. I feel exhausted, emotionally drained."

Jack watched her leave and then reached for the bottle of Scotch. He poured another shot, sat back, and contemplated a day that had started badly, gotten worse, and then really gone downhill.

32

JACK WAS SPRAWLED ACROSS the sofa when he woke to the sound of the phone ringing. He rose, hurried to the desk, and said, "Jack Anderson."

"This is Duncan Pike."

"I was sleeping. What's the time?"

"Quarter past eleven."

"It's been a long evening for you."

"Long and demanding. The Baxters are not easy customers."

"Where do we stand?"

"We have an offer that they say is final. It includes an agreement to sign a contract that I would construct with every possible safeguard for Georgie, her daughter, and you. I told them the contract has to be part of the settlement, and they didn't quibble."

"Is that because they don't intend to honour it?"

"No, I take it as the reverse. They'll accept the contract

because they have no interest in you or Georgie once they've got their money."

"How much money?"

"That's what took so long to sort out," Pike said. "Do you know how much Atholl Malcolm stole from them?"

"No."

"Three and a half million pounds."

"Do you believe that?"

"Actually, I do."

"That's more than five million dollars."

"Yes, and that doesn't count the forty thousand pounds they've spent trying to track him down."

"How much do they want from me?"

"One million pounds."

Jack caught his breath. "One and a half million dollars."

"Yes, thereabouts," Pike said. "They started off asking for it all, and of course I counter-offered two hundred and fifty thousand. After quite a bit of back-and-forth, I eventually got them down to one million."

"That's an awful lot of money."

"What were you expecting?"

"The two hundred and fifty thousand you started with would have been at the high end."

"Well, one million is the best I could do, and I'm not going back to them. You might find solace in this: they've agreed to pay you back with the first million they collect from Malcolm, if he's ever found," Pike said. "I added that on the assumption that he might eventually contact Georgie or her daughter."

"What if we find Malcolm and he's broke?"

"Nothing ventured, nothing gained."

"So that's it? That's the whole deal?"

"It is. What will you do?"

"How long do I have to decide?"

"The clock is ticking. They wanted an answer by midnight tonight, but I managed to put them off until noon tomorrow."

"I need to do some thinking," Jack said.

"My advice to you is not to overthink this. You're prepared to pay one million pounds or you're not. There's no more negotiating to be done. If your answer is yes, I'll put together the most fearsome contract Glasgow has ever seen, and maybe when you get home you can turn your security team loose to find Malcolm. If it's no . . . Well, then, we all live with the consequences."

"I understand my choices. You'll hear from me by noon tomorrow."

"Make it eleven. I'd prefer not to cut it so close."

"Okay, I'll call you by then," Jack said.

Jack slumped over the desk. A million and a half dollars was more than he'd paid for his house, and that was the most expensive purchase of his life. Now he was being asked to pay a small fortune to save a woman he'd met only four days ago. Hell, a week ago he hadn't even known she existed. And what about Harry? Why hadn't the Baxters gone after him? Why hadn't Harry offered to solve his sister's problem? Why did it all have to fall on him? What did he owe these people? Not a goddamn thing. In fact, they'd already cost him the chance to stay on at Pilgrim. And now he was expected to pay a million and a half dollars.

"Fuck," he said, picking up the phone. "Why should I?"

"Jack, is that you?" Harry answered.

"Yes. Is Georgie available?"

"She's upstairs resting, but I can get her."

"I think you should."

"Is there news?"

"Not yet. I'm still working on it."

"I'll get Georgie," Harry said, his disappointment apparent.

While he waited, Jack retrieved the Scotch bottle from the coffee table and filled his glass with the last of its contents. Strangely, given how much he'd consumed, he didn't feel drunk.

"Jack, this is Georgie," she finally said, her voice strained.

"Hi. Listen, I'm trying to get this situation resolved, and I have a couple of questions."

"Go ahead."

"Please don't take this the wrong way, but do you swear neither you nor Liz knows where Atholl could be?"

"We don't have a clue."

"Neither of you have heard from him, not even a word?"

"No."

"If Liz had, would she tell you?"

"Of course. She knows how much it would mean to me."

"One more thing. You told me a few days ago that if you knew where he was, you would be prepared to tell the Baxters. After what they did to you, do you still feel that way?"

"Truthfully, I don't know. I might, I guess, but I don't feel as sure about that as I did."

"Thanks for being so honest," he said. "Now try to rest. I am working on our problem. By tomorrow we'll know where we stand."

He checked the time and knew that Atlas Travel in Wellesley would still be open. "I have no choice," he muttered as he took their travel itinerary from his jacket pocket, found Atlas's number and dialled.

"Atlas Travel. This is Miriam," a woman answered.

"This is Jack Anderson. My wife, Anne, and I are in Scotland right now. We booked our flights through you."

"Yes, Mr. Anderson. I remember doing that for you."

"We're in Edinburgh and we need to get home as quickly as possible."

"I'm so sorry to hear that."

"Yes. Well, I'd like you to find two first-class seats out of Glasgow or Edinburgh as early as possible tomorrow. I don't care about the cost. We just need to get home."

"I can do that for you. Shall I call you with options?"

"Go ahead and book the one you think looks best, then call me at this hotel. Here's the number," he said.

His blazer was hung over the back of the chair. As he put the itinerary back in the pocket, he felt its paper catch against something. He reached into the pocket and pulled out the two photos Georgie had given him. He stared at the one with Jessie on the sand dunes, barely comprehending that he had been that boy. Why were they in Irvine? What was he pointing the stick at? Why was she smiling so broadly? What had made them so happy?

He put that photo aside and turned to the second one, of him and Moira with their mother. Jessie looked like a different person. No, she *was* a different person. She was still in her mid-twenties but looked ravaged and pitiful. He looked more closely at his face and Moira's. Those weren't happy children. Their smiles were cautious and guarded, as if they were harbouring secrets. What did he actually remember of his childhood? As hard as he tried, he couldn't conjure up a single memory of his life before the movie theatre. Everything and everyone was blacked out. It was as if his life had begun when he was abandoned. That memory was there, vivid and burning, and nothing else.

"I should be able to remember something, but there's nothing," he muttered.

"Nothing where?" Anne asked.

"How long have you been standing there?"

"A few seconds. Can I join you?"

"Sure," he said. "I was looking at the photos Georgie gave me."

"When I saw what your mother wrote on the back, I felt like crying," Anne said as she came over to stand next to him.

"Because she referred to me as Bonnie Jack? Please," he said derisively.

"Why would you say that?"

"If she really loved me, she would never have done what she did. You heard Moira and Georgie; she was trying to survive that monster we met two days ago. Yet she saw fit to leave me with him. She didn't just abandon me; she tried to turn me over to him. What would have happened if he'd taken me? Why does no one think about that?"

"You've had more to drink," Anne said.

"So what. I also had a nap. My mind is functioning just fine."

"And you've decided not to help Georgie," Anne said. "I can tell by the way you're talking about your mother. And I can see it in your eyes — those eyes that won't look directly at me."

"How can you possibly tell what I'm thinking?"

"Then tell me I'm wrong."

He brushed past her and walked to the window. "Pike called. The Baxters want one and a half million dollars to let Georgie off the hook."

"That's a lot of money. But we have it, and more if we need it."

"One and a half million dollars to help a woman we've known for just four days?"

"She's your sister."

"So she says. How do we know that McPherson really was her father?"

"What does that matter? There's no doubt about her mother. When I met Liz and saw those pictures of Jessie when she was young, I saw our Allison, and I knew. You can't be that blind."

"Maybe I am."

"I want to change the subject," she said abruptly. "What does Pike say we get for a million and a half?"

"Supposedly Georgie gets off the hook. But who really knows? The Baxters could come back for more."

"You say that without much conviction. Does Pike think they might?"

"He'd get them to sign a contract saying they won't. Six months from now it could be worth nothing."

"Or it could stick."

"Jesus, Anne, why are you pushing so hard for this?"

She walked to the window, wrapped her arms around his waist, and pressed her face into his back. "When I was lying in bed, I was thinking about our children and the family we've created. Family was something I was missing until I met you. Where would we be without our kids or each other? Now we have a chance to expand that family, and we'll all be the better for it if we do. Jack, I like these people."

"But they're hardly *real* family."

"I don't understand you. You had a hole in your life that you sought to fill by coming here. Georgie had one in hers that she wanted to fill by finding McPherson and you. Moira was a disappointment and McPherson was a disaster, but so what? Things may not work out with Georgie and Harry, but we shouldn't let money get in the way of trying."

"Anne, we're talking about a million and a half dollars."

She pushed back from him and stepped away. "Is this really about the money?"

"What are you getting at?

"I don't think you can forgive your mother for abandoning you, and I don't think you can reconcile your pain with the feelings Georgie has for her. Are you really prepared to turn your back on Georgie just because the two of you have differing views about your mother? Because if you are, you'll be doing to her and Liz what your mother did to you—and with much less reason."

"That's nonsense."

"Jack, don't make me ashamed of you. I don't think I can live with a man I'm ashamed of."

33

JACK AND ANNE'S PAN-AM flight from Prestwick landed at Boston's Logan Airport at three in the afternoon. By the time they'd cleared Customs and retrieved their luggage, it was four and rush hour was underway.

They had slept off and on for most of the flight, exhausted physically and emotionally by their last days in Scotland. As their limo crept towards the Callahan Tunnel under Boston Harbor, Jack said, "We'll be at least an hour, probably longer, getting to Wellesley."

"There's no rush. We have no plans except to get caught up on sleep," Anne said.

"I'm so tired I can barely think."

"You have two days at home before you have to go back to work."

"That isn't something I'm excited about."

"The two days at home?"

"No, going back to work. It's always been my domain,

my sanctuary, and now I don't know what I'll find," he said. "I'm afraid that story in the *Tribune*, and the way I handled it, has taken a toll."

Anne started to say something comforting and then stopped herself. The limo was in the tunnel now, crawling forward in its eerie light.

"I thought at least one of the kids might have come to the airport to meet us," he said. "I looked for them when we walked into the arrivals area. It was disappointing not to see anyone."

"I was watching for them as well, but that was a bit much to expect. We changed our schedule at the last minute, and they all have active lives in other cities."

Traffic was bumper to bumper as they emerged from the tunnel. When their limo finally reached the Mass Pike, however, traffic became less congested and they started moving slowly and steadily towards the western suburbs.

They drove past Allston, Brighton, and Cambridge. When they reached the Watertown-Newton exit, Jack said, "Every time I go by here I think of Martin and Colleen. Over the years, that's thousands and thousands of times. You don't realize unless you stop to think about it just how much of your life is filled with thoughts about your family, alive and dead."

"I know. There isn't a day that goes by when I don't think about our children," Anne said. "And on the plane I thought more than once about Georgie and Liz. I hope they're okay."

"Pike is confident that the Baxters will stick to the deal. I trust his judgement."

She reached for his hand. "It was good of you to change your mind."

"In the end, it was the right thing to do."

"Excuse me," the driver said as they passed Newton, "do you want me to take the Wellesley exit and Route Nine or the Weston exit and Route Thirty?"

"Take Nine. I know it's slower, but I rather want to see the town. It will make me feel like I'm really home," Anne said, and then turned to Jack. "That's the route the kids always want me to take when they come home."

Traffic wasn't bad, and ten minutes later the limo made a right turn at the train station onto Cliff Road. Jack directed the driver towards Pierce and the final turn onto Monadnock. As their house loomed into view, Anne gasped and reached for Jack's hand. "That's Brent's car in the driveway. He must have driven up from New York."

The limo pulled into the driveway, and Anne's hand was on the door handle before it came to a full stop. She jumped out and started running towards the house. When she reached the steps, the front door opened. Brent stood in the opening, with Maggie next to him. Behind them she could see Allison and Mark. Anne stood there frozen, tears welling up in her eyes.

"Welcome home!" Brent shouted, and the others joined the chorus.

Anne began to cry in earnest. Her children clambered

down the steps and surrounded her. Allison pulled her in close and hugged her. Anne was sobbing now, her shoulders heaving.

Jack approached, carrying their bags. He put them down when he reached the children. "You surprised us," he said, his voice thick with emotion.

It took a while for the family to untangle and file into the house, where they gathered in the kitchen, taking their usual seats on the benches around the pine rectory table.

"We made a cheese plate, there's cold white wine in the fridge, and Mark brought a very fine bottle of Scotch," Allison said.

"Why don't we save it for later," Anne said, still teary. "Your father and I had so much to drink in the past week that we're about ready to float away."

"As true as that is," Jack said, "I will try Mark's Scotch."

"Oh. In that case, I will have some wine," Anne said.

When Mark and Maggie got up to get the drinks, Allison said, "Tony is sorry he couldn't make it. His schedule is jammed."

"We understand. We didn't make it easy with our flight change."

Drinks were poured and distributed. Brent lifted his glass. "Cheers, and welcome home," he said.

Everyone drank, but then an awkward silence fell over the table. The children looked at each other questioningly, and then Maggie asked loudly, "Who's going to start?"

"I guess we should," Anne said after a slight hesitation.

"What's been going on?" Mark asked.

"Your father and I had an adventure," Anne said. "To call it a trip doesn't do it justice, but we're here now, safe and sound, and Dad isn't in jail, so I guess everything worked out in the end."

"Tell us all about it," said Allison.

"I'd like your dad to do that."

For the next half-hour Jack described their visit with Moira; their excursions to his mother's grave and the Glasgow movie theatre; the first meetings with Harry, Barbara, and Georgie; and Georgie's stories about McPherson's treatment of their mother. When he mentioned Liz, Anne interrupted. "I have a photo of her. Let me show you," she said, getting up from the table and going over to her handbag. She handed it to Brent. "What do you think?" she asked.

"It looks like Allison when she was younger," he said.

"But it isn't. It's Liz."

"Let me see that," Allison said. She stared at the photo, looked away, and then returned to it. "Oh my god, that hair. I didn't think anyone had hair like mine."

"She's an actress, and quite talented. She's part of the ensemble at the Pitlochry Festival this summer. Dad and I are going back to give her some support," Anne said. "It would be terrific if you all could join us. But if you can't, you'll get to meet her anyway. We've invited the entire Scottish branch of the family to come stay with us for Thanksgiving."

"It'll be crowded, but we'll find a way to fit everyone in," Jack said.

"Your father has some other photos, but I think he should save those for later," Anne said as Liz's photo was being passed around the table. "Why don't you pick up our adventure where you left off."

"Before I start, I'd like to get another drink."

"Me too," Brent said.

After fresh drinks were served, Jack picked up the story. "I need to tell you about Atholl Malcolm, Georgie's husband." He then recounted the story of Malcolm's business practices, his flight from Scotland, and Georgie and Liz's subsequent humiliations.

"It turned out that Malcolm had stolen about five million dollars from the Baxter brothers," Jack said. "They hadn't been able to locate him and had no hope of recovering their money until they saw the story about me in the *Tribune*."

"They wanted you to pay what Malcolm owed? Five million dollars?" Brent asked.

"That's right."

"They asked you directly?"

"No, the approach was made through Georgie," he said. "They threatened to hurt her if I didn't co-operate. Duncan Pike knows the Baxters, and when I asked him if he thought the threats were real, he said it was likely they were."

"Did you go to the police?"

"No. We were told that it would only anger the Baxters and place Georgie and Liz in a vulnerable position. So I decided to forego the police and do a deal with the Baxters, through Pike," Jack said. "We closed it yesterday."

"Are Georgie and Liz safe now?" Allison asked.

"We think so, or at least Pike does. And I was telling Mom in the car that I trust his judgement."

"Thank goodness," Allison said.

Anne smiled at her children. "So that was our adventure. What do you think?"

"Amazing," Allison said. "And I can't get over that picture of Liz."

"I have other pictures, but before I show them to you, I'd like Dad to show you one."

Jack looked at her questioningly. "The one of you and your mother at the beach," she said to him.

He went to his blazer where it was hanging on a hook and took the photo from his pocket. He sat down before giving it to Allison.

Allison stared at the photo, looked at her father, and stared at it again. "I look so much like her it's eerie," she said.

"You do. She was a pretty woman until life turned against her," he said.

"And Dad, you were such a handsome little boy," said Allison.

"Turn over the photo and read what's on the back," Anne said.

Allison read, "'July 1931, an outing to the Irvine shore with my Bonnie Jack.'"

"He's Bonnie Jack now," Anne said. "That's what his mother called him, that's what Georgie calls him, and that's what I'm going to call him—whether he likes it or not."

"Bonnie Jack," Allison said, and then looked at her father. "Dad, what do you think? I know you hate your other nickname. Can you live with this one?"

"Anything is better than Bloody Jack," he said.

34

THEY LAY WRAPPED IN each other's arms, her breath gently tickling his neck.

"I'm so tired I can't sleep," Jack said.

"Me too. What are you thinking?" Anne asked.

"I'm thinking about the kids. Did you notice that not· one of them doubted we'd done the right thing by paying off the Baxters to leave Georgie and Liz in peace?"

"I wasn't surprised."

"And no one asked how much I paid. Plenty of people would have been angry about part of their inheritance being given away like that."

"We didn't raise selfish children."

"You mean *you* didn't raise selfish children."

"You did your part, Jack. Stop being so hard on yourself."

He was quiet for a moment as he assessed her words.

"And there are people who would have been mortified

to see their father's name and picture splashed across the front page of a tabloid, because he killed an old man in a pub. Our kids took it all in stride."

"They know what kind of man you are, and they're all proud of you."

"They wouldn't have been if I'd left Georgie and Liz to the mercy of the Baxters," he said. "And you know that was what I was intending."

"You were confused, that's all. You would have made the right decision eventually."

"I'm not so sure. If you hadn't forced the issue . . ."

"Jack, please stop," Anne said. "You were tired, you were drinking, and you'd been through an emotional wringer."

"Even if all that is true, I can't help feeling that the weakest part of my character took over," Jack said. "I remember telling Georgie and Harry on the way to meet McPherson that I'm too often selfish, too often self-absorbed. And that's how I was acting until you intervened."

"All I did was remind you about the man you are."

"Don't you mean you reminded me about who you believe I am?"

"If you say so."

"Well, it doesn't matter. The bottom line is, you scared the hell out of me."

"How?"

"You said you couldn't live with a man you're ashamed of," he said. "Tell me, would you have left me if I hadn't helped Georgie?"

"What do you think?"

He hugged her tightly. "I thought you would. That's why I was so scared."

"Then let's leave it at that."

Acknowledgements

My father's life was the genesis of this book. Abandoned by his mother in a movie house as a boy, he kept the fact that he had a sister a secret for more than fifty years. He informed the family — including my very surprised mother — at a dinner. A few months later, he flew to England to visit the sister. It did not go well, and he never saw her again. But over the course of that meeting, she informed him he had two other siblings, a full sister and a half sister. He eventually met with them, and with his full sister he managed to establish an arm's length relationship.

Transforming my bricklayer father into an insurance executive was my way of providing him with a voice for the feelings he could never express.

Jack's use of the U.K. National Health Service as a source of information to locate his sister Moira (or anyone else) is not something I believe — especially in these years of privacy protection — the NHS would respond positively to. I'm not sure it was that way in 1988, and my father's quite specific recollection was of writing a letter to the NHS seeking information about his sister, and of getting a reply that led him to her. Whether or not his description of events was accurate, I decided to maintain his memory of it.

I have written more than fifteen books in two crime/thriller series, but I did not approach writing this novel with any sense of confidence. Obviously, I knew I could finish it, but I wasn't sure it would be of the quality I wanted. My wife, Lorraine, is usually my first reader, but for this book I added another: Douglas Gibson, Canada's editor emeritus. Doug graciously agreed to read the first draft and give me his opinion. What I wanted—rather presumptuously—was an answer to the question "Is the book worth publishing?" If Doug had expressed any reservations, I would have put the manuscript in a drawer and left it there. Instead, he was complimentary, as was Lorraine, and the book was sent to my publisher, House of Anansi, where another Doug (Richmond, my editor) accepted it for publication.

So a big thanks to the two Dougs, and of course to Lorraine.

Lastly, I have never hesitated to use other people's clever sayings in my books, but I have also made a habit of giving proper recognition to the source. In the Ava books, the saying "People always do the right thing for the wrong reason" was attributed to Saul Alinsky. In this book, Anne Anderson says, "Think twice before you have something to say, and then don't say it." I don't know if our family friend Claudette Mikelsons invented that line, but she is the only person I've ever heard utter it, and so I'm giving her the credit.

IAN HAMILTON is the author of thirteen novels in the Ava Lee series and three in the Lost Decades of Uncle Chow Tung series. His books have been shortlisted for numerous prizes, including the Arthur Ellis Award, the Barry Award, and the Lambda Literary Prize, and are national bestsellers. BBC Culture named Hamilton one of the ten mystery/ crime writers from the past thirty years who should be on your bookshelf. The Ava Lee series is being adapted for television.